CAPTAIN SCULLY

DUNCAN JEFFERSON

Printed in the United States of America
First Printing, 2018

Printed in the USA

Cover by Jenn Reece at
WWW.TIGERBRIGHTSTUDIOS.COM
Interior design and typesetting by Ampersand Book Interiors
WWW.AMPERSANDBOOKINTERIORS.COM

9 8 7 6 5 4 3 2 1

PAPERBACK - 978-0-6480694-9-2

ALSO BY
DUNCAN JEFFERSON

Mr. Dickens

Camino Salvado: A Pilgrimage

CONTENTS

This is the place. Stand still, my steed,
Let me review the scene,
And summon from the shadowy Past
The forms that once have been.

—Henry Wadsworth Longfellow
From 'A gleam of sunshine', 1845

PREFACE

I CAME ACROSS CAPTAIN JOHN SCULLY whilst exploring a walking track between the city of Perth in Western Australia and the monastery town of New Norcia some 180 kilometres to the north. I became intrigued as to why, in the early part of the nineteenth century, a single, young Irishman should come to be the most isolated settler in the fledgling Swan River Settlement.

In researching his story I came to discover other amazing adventurers, explorers and missionaries who were drawn to that remote community and who connected Scully to kings, queens, popes and even saints.

John Scully might have been a solitary figure but he lived in a time when the world was changing beyond all recognition. Yet he also lived amongst some of the most ancient peoples on the planet – the Aboriginal people of Australia. This is partly their story too, albeit a sadder one as they were dispossessed of the land they loved so much.

Whilst researching John Scully I received much help from the State Libraries of Western Australia and New South Wales. The Trove archives of Australian newspapers also proved invaluable for tracking John Scully in both New South Wales and the fledgling Swan River Settlement. I am indebted to Julie Rae, who provided me with some of the early maps showing where John Scully first took up land near York and Toodyay. Finding information about the Irish part of the story proved more of a challenge but I was greatly helped by Beatrice Doran in Dublin.

I made an early decision to reach as many people as I could, which is why I introduced the fictional character of Frankie Scully into the story. It then became apparent that the book was going in two different directions and I am indebted to Canadian author Michael Redhill, winner of the Giller Prize, who reviewed my original manuscript and gave me great encouragement and wise advice. And of course, I owe a lifelong debt to my wife Maggie who accompanied me in my search and was patient with me in my long silences.

Duncan Jefferson
Perth, Western Australia
March 2018

ONE

Ireland

IT WAS A TERRIBLE CROSSING. STORMS and high winds plagued us all the way across the Atlantic. Now here we were nudging our way along the Irish coast as the captain of the liner probed the thick fog in an attempt to find Dublin.

For the whole journey across, our vessel, the SS *Egypt*, had pitched and lurched constantly with predictable consequences for the great majority of its passengers. We had embarked in New York with high hopes, a holiday atmosphere pervading all the decks. The ship itself was barely half full, even in steerage, which added to the festive feeling upon the vessel. Thankfully I had my own cabin, meaning I had no other person to bother me for the start of my exile, and believe me, I fully intended to enjoy myself as much as I could for as long as I could.

Being the youngest of five sons had led my mother to indulge me a little more than perhaps she ought. But then she died and our world changed. If her mollycoddling had made me somewhat of a spoiled brat whilst she was alive, after she passed, I became a sulky, spoiled brat! In fact, those were the precise words my father used when reading me the riot act, a ritual he found necessary to perform with monotonous regularity. Eventually he told me that he had had enough and that I should learn to stand on my own two feet. I was of an age to study and as there were few opportunities presenting themselves near our ranch in Nebraska, it was about time I left home and took life seriously. His idea was for me to study law, to preserve the faint hope that at some point in the future I might be of some use in the family business.

Behind my sulking exterior I was secretly delighted. Being a playboy on the plains was beginning to drain even my fertile imagination. But Pa had a twist in the tail of his great plan that dampened my delight. I was to study at Trinity College in Dublin, where he and many of his family had studied. 'If you can't grow up there, then there's little hope for you, my boy', he said, looking up at me from the other side of his great oak desk.

'Yes, Sir', was all I could find to reply to him. Ireland had not played any part in my plans, and without Mom to rescue me I knew my fate was sealed.

Mom had been as different from Pa as chalk is from cheese. Where he was all drive and burning ambition, she was shy and frail; too frail, in fact. She came from gentile New York stock and had been swept off her feet by the fiery Irishman with his dreams and wealth. Life out on the plains was hard on her and many's the time she went to visit with her family in New York for months on end, leaving Pa to corral his wild and wilful boys. At heart she had been soft and gentle and kind, and I liked to think that perhaps I had inherited a few of her characteristics along with the stubborn streak of my single-minded father.

Sometimes just thinking about him made me mad! 'Bastard', I muttered to myself as I clung to the damp rail of the *Egypt*, pulling the lapels of my greatcoat close around my neck. It still smelled of vomit, which did nothing to improve my mood. That nauseating miasma had been the result of my attempting to seduce Mary Nash, a pretty young thing from steerage who could not hold her sherry. I had enticed her to my cabin in her intoxicated state, but the combination of the sweet sherry and the rolling of the ship had led her to vomit all over my cabin. The smell of it now clung to all my clothes like a shellac of guilt.

I stared into the impenetrable fog and listened for the low groan of the foghorn groping its way out of the gloom from the lighthouse near Dún Laoghaire. A sudden shout went up from a fellow passenger: 'There it is. Over there at about 11 o'clock! You can just make out the light through the fog.' As if on cue, there was a lifting of the gloom and the silken beam of the beacon shone clearly toward us. We heard the waves lapping against the harbour wall and then everything briefly came into view. The solid stone walls glistened with wetness, and then disappeared into the greyness. The fog muffled the voices of the dockside workers with their strong brogues as they retrieved ropes and fastened the ship close adding to the ghostliness of the scene.

'I'm sorry about your coat', a small voice whispered to me from my elbow. Mary had crept up from her deck clutching her bundle of belongings. She was a fragile waif now that I looked at her closely through more sober eyes.

'Is the weather always like this in Dublin?'

'Oh no', she replied earnestly. 'It rains a lot, too', and she stared at me with her wide blue eyes. Before I had mustered my wits, Mary laughed gaily and went on. 'Seriously, it should never have happened so let's forget it, eh?' She held out her hand to me. 'Friends?' I took her small hand in mine and grunted something in reply.

'If you're ever walking by the Coombe, just ask for Mary Nash', she said. 'That's if you want to.' Her expression both pleased and gently mocked me. 'I'll say a wee prayer for you', she added. 'Something tells me you might need it.' The expression in her eyes stayed with me long after she had turned on her heel and left. I watched her walk toward the doorway where the hungry mouth of the stairwell swallowed her up.

I suddenly noticed the explosion of bustle and noise all over the ship. People whom I had not seen during the voyage appeared from their cabins looking frail and pale from the trauma of their excursion. People with great and small cases edged through narrow passages and pushed others out of their way. Small children clung to the coats of bigger folk and drank in the unfolding chaos that confronted them. Orders were yelled and orders were ignored. People pushed and shoved to try and disembark a few minutes faster, only to descend into the larger cauldron of humanity waiting to greet them dockside.

I reached into my inside pocket and pulled out a silver cigarette case. It was my father's but I had told myself that he would not miss it as he had several. Tapping the cigarette on the side of the case and trying to look suave and worldly, I struck a fizzing match and inhaled the blue tobacco smoke deep into my lungs. Thinking back, it was a dumb thing to do. Who was going to be impressed? Everyone was far too pre-occupied to worry about a flashy man about town like me. But heads did turn as I broke out into a paroxysm of coughing, which caused me to retch over the side of the boat. 'Oy!' came a yell from below. 'If you're going to be sick, at least vomit over the water and not down here among the people, you great eejit.' I stamped out the offending object and retreated sheepishly to my cabin to prepare for my disembarkation.

My trunk had been placed on the bunk by the steward. I gathered my travelling clothes together and bundled them into it. Already in the trunk were my treasures from home: books, letters and a framed photograph of our family taken outside of the ranch in Kansas. I picked it up and rubbed the glass with the sleeve of my greatcoat. Seeing them all look so regimented made me smile. Behind them all, the ranch house looked dwarfed by the Great Plains rolling into the distance behind it.

The Kansas house was our autumn home. Although we loved it, during the summer months it was far too hot to consider staying there. Summertime was when the winds blew across the landscape, burnishing everything brown with its desiccating heat. But it was not just the summer heat that made the place unbearable; there were the twisters that grew out of massive storm clouds and funnelled everything in their path a mile high into the sky and spreading the detroitus across the landscape. I had experienced a few in my life and they sent shivers of dread through me, even here in damp old Dublin.

The lid of the trunk closed with a loud crack and I secured it with an iron padlock. My uncle's address had already been painted on the top, so after a brief check around the cabin, I pulled the door closed behind me and left. I was in no great hurry to leave the ship because the thought of moving into a cramped damp room in this waterlogged city held no joy for me whatsoever.

Naturally, I had some knowledge of my uncle but it was scanty and did not fill me with any expectations of a good time. John Scully was already in his late seventies and his wife Maria not that much younger. They had no children, so it looked like there would be no break from the tedium of their age or from their devotion to their Catholic faith. My exile from America was beginning to seem more like prison sentance than a chance to experience life.

I gave instructions to a porter on the dockside and gave him a silver crown. He tipped his cap, and before he went off in search of my trunk, asked if I would like him to arrange a cab. I told him that I preferred to walk. ''Tis a grand day for a walk, Sir', came his bright reply. 'Nice and soft for the skin and be-dad it'll be clear by noon if mi auld bones read the weather right.' Having delivered this auspicious prediction he limped off up the gangplank and disappeared into the bowels of the boat.

I struck out along the long Dún Laoghaire pier in the direction of Anglesea Road. I knew the way well, having studied it closely on the map my father had provided. But what the map did not show were the potholes and the mud that caked everything. Soon my boots and the lower fringe of my greatcoat were the same colour as my environment.

It was a good hour's walk through those dirty streets before I stood at the gate outside of number 25. I should not have been surprised by what I saw, as most of the houses I had walked past were of a similar construction. Two stories high with grey slate roofs and built with bilious red bricks. Large bay windows seemed to bloat out from either side of the front door. I found myself in front of the large brass door-knocker. Taking a deep breath I lifted the solid dolphin by the head and let it fall with a loud clank against the wooden door. I waited, staring at the painted wood in front of me. I was investigating a strange metal structure low down to one side of the door when I heard the handle turn and found my uncle standing in the doorway.

'It's for scraping mud off your boots', were his first words to me. 'So I suggest you use it before you come in.' Having made this pronouncement, he turned and went down the papered hallway and into a room on his left. I flicked up the heel of my boots and discovered that he had been correct in his assumption about the mud. Whilst I was removing it I made up my mind that at the first opportunity I would need to get as far away as possible from this sad old place.

Satisfied that my boots were clean enough, I went in. As the door closed behind me I had a strange premonition. It was as if one half of me wanted to immediately run out of that claustrophobic mausoleum, and yet another part was intrigued by what I might find there. True, there was the smell of stale cooking from the kitchen, which I presumed was at the far end of the hallway, but on the walls there were artefacts I had never seen before in my life. I took off my coat and hung it on one of the pegs next to other, older coats. A large black cane with garish colours had been left carelessly in the corner behind the door. I was about to take a closer look when my uncle appeared again, saying, 'Well, are you coming in or not?'

I followed him into the room and spoke my first words to him. 'Francis Scully, Sir. I'm pleased to make your acquaintance. Most people call me Frankie back home'. I proffered my hand for him to shake it. For what was perhaps just a few moments we stood there exploring each other's faces, then he took my hand in a surprisingly strong grip and responded, 'John Scully. Welcome to Dublin city.' He searched my face as if seeking out familiar landmarks. 'You have a bit of your father in you. How is he? Well, I hope?'

'Very well indeed, Sir. He said to extend his best regards and hopes to see you in the near future. He has some land business to attend to here which will demand his presence soon', I replied as tactfully as I could. John Scully's smile was like the heat of a candle; if you were too far away you would miss it. But when you did see it you felt happy inside.

'Sit down, lad.' He pointed to a chair on one side of the bay window. 'Maria is out and about playing cards with her cronies so no doubt we'll have the rest of the day to ourselves.' John sat down and looked out of the window as if he was seeing something that others could not. He was not as big as I had pictured him to be but perhaps he had just shrunk with age. His face was open and frank and framed by white bushy side-burns, which were the fashion of the times. His clear blue eyes were filmed by a skim of skin that appeared to be spearing out from the inner corner. The exposed skin on his face held few visible lines but here and there scaly red patches suggested that perhaps he suffered from some form of irritating rash.

'Too much sun in the antipodes', he said, as if reading my mind, whilst picking the flakes off one of the patches. 'It's not something you see too often here in Ireland though.' He turned his gaze back to me, asking, 'So, how was the crossing?'

'Turbulent, Sir, would be the best way to describe it. Most passengers never left their cabins so the social life was pretty quiet.' I forced a smile but received none in return. I took the opportunity to glance around the room. It was small by

American standards and felt cramped. A coal fire burned low in the grate and gave off sufficient heat to warm us in our chairs. Heavy dark drapes were marshalled at either side of the window which leaked in the low light through white net curtains. The sound of a gas lamp hissed above the fireplace and sent its sallow light into the room, no doubt giving me the same jaundiced complexion as it was giving John Scully.

'I'm afraid you'll find this a great change from what you're used to, Frankie', he said. But further conversation was interrupted by a loud rap from the decorative brass dolphin. 'That's your trunk, I expect', he said, rising from his chair. 'We'll get that and then I'll show you to your room.'

'Thank you, Sir', I replied, rising at the same time. John paused by the door.

'The last time someone called me Sir, I was letting him off a fine for urinating in public during my time as a magistrate in Oughterard. It's not a pleasant memory so please call me John.' I took a deep breath and muttered to myself, 'This is going to be hard', before following him to retrieve my belongings.

My room was to be the guest room on the first floor. I was to learn that many such houses in Ireland have spare room which they keep especially for 'guests'. The common denominator is that since guests, or indeed anyone, rarely venture into them, they all give the sensation of entering a state of suspended animation. To compound this frigid atmosphere most of them have no heating, but thankfully this was not the case in mine! The porter helped me carry my trunk up the narrow staircase, along the little landing and into my room. He received some extra copper coins for his help and left promising to, 'Drink your health, Surr.'

'I'll leave you to it and go and put the kettle on', my uncle said, closing the door behind him. I sat on the bed and patted the thick layer of blankets that had been put on, especially for me, no doubt. I was pleasantly surprised at how light and friendly the room felt. The window overlooked the rear of the house, the River Dodder and the parkland around it. At that time of year the trees were all bare, so the feeling of wide open spaces – despite the inevitable greyness of everything – lifted my drooping spirits. A small fire had been lit which added to the cosiness, and the papered walls were not over-fussy as is often the case in such dwellings.

A five drawer dresser stood behind the door and was made of a wood that I had never seen before. It was almost cherry red and extremely heavy. Above it hung an old photograph of a red sailed dinghy on what looked like a vast lake. Small hills fringed the expanse of water and I could just make out a cluster of low buildings in the distance. But the trees and vegetation were like nothing that I had seen before. I wondered if it could be Australia, knowing something of my uncle's past.

Just past the entrance to the room was a tall mahogany wardrobe with a full length mirror on its narrow door. The mirror reflected the light from the window, adding to the gaiety of the room. I looked at myself in the mirror and smiled for the first time in a few days. Maybe this wasn't going to be so bad after all.

Unpacking was swiftly completed and I soon gazed into the empty depths of the trunk wondering where I should put it. I closed the lid and took my question downstairs and laid it before my uncle.

'Well, I doubt you'd get it up into the loft', he said, stirring the pot before placing a knitted cosy over it. 'But there's plenty of room in the shed down the garden if you're not too worried about it getting damp.'

'That's fine by me, John', I replied, pulling up a chair by the kitchen table. John remained with his back to me by the cooking range as he replaced the tea caddy and pulled down some mugs from the shelves above it.

'Maria will not be happy with me for not getting out the best china', he said over his shoulder. 'You don't mind, do you?'

'No, Sir. Sorry, John. No, that's fine by me.'

'Fine it is, then', he said, bringing the mugs and the tea to the table and pulling out a chair of his own. We both looked out of the kitchen window and into the rear garden. The heat in the room was womb-like and I felt as if this was the real part of the house where real people lived and talked. I sipped on the tea and it was hot, very hot!

'Back home we drink our tea iced, John, but I must admit that in this country...' I left the sentence unfinished as I slurped some more of the hot brown liquid. John shrugged his shoulders as he lifted his mug to his mouth and looked across its steaming rim at me.

'Cousin William's made a bit of a name for himself, hasn't he?' he asked with one eyebrow raised. 'How much land has he got now? It's a pity he's not as popular back here in Ireland. Is that why he sent you over? To find out how the land lies, so to speak?'

'You have to be joking!' I exclaimed. 'Father wouldn't trust me with anything that important. I'm afraid you've got the black sheep of the family, John. I've been sent here on a shape up or ship out mission.' I couldn't help letting out a sigh of frustration. 'He wants me to go to Trinity, become a great lawyer and then sort out all the legal stuff for the family in the years ahead.' Silence ensued as we both cupped our hot mugs and looked out into the garden gloom.

'So, did you have any adventures whilst you were in the high seas?' John changed the subject deftly. 'When I first went to sea we didn't have too many luxuries. No big steam-driven turbines back then. Just the wind and the canvas.' He was watching me all the time that he spoke. 'Sounds romantic doesn't it?'

'Sure does. What sort of ship did you sail on?' I asked, only half interested in the reply. 'Did you get sea sick? Half the people on the *Egypt* spent the voyage vomiting out their portholes, so romantic it was not!'

'Do you really want to hear what it was like?' he asked in return. 'Or are you just trying to be nice to an old man in his own home?' Those eyes of his gleamed at me. 'Don't answer that', he added quietly. 'When I was your age the last thing I'd have wanted was to be in the company of an old man like me. Still, beggars can't be choosers and the weather being what it is, why don't we add a speck of rum to our tea and tell a few tales, eh?' The mention of alcohol flicked a switch in my attention.

'I've never been known to refuse a drink, John, but I have to admit that rum isn't a drink I'm too familiar with where I come from.'

John's smile wreathed his face. 'By the cut of you, my lad, I reckon you'll soon get the hang of it. But go easy. We don't want the lady of the house thinking that I've been leading you into temptation, do we?' He rose from his chair, scraping it along the bare, tiled kitchen floor. Mounting it, he climbed up to a high cupboard and pushed some empty storage jars out of the way before retrieving a half-empty bottle of dark rum. Descending gingerly, he said with a grin, 'It would be a dreadful shame if I fell and broke anything, wouldn't it?' He un-screwed the cap and poured a healthy glug of rum into my tea.

'*Sláinte*', I said and we clinked mugs together. The bite of the rum added to the heat of the tea, multiplying its warming effect and immediately putting me at ease.

'Tell me about your first trip, John. Any nice ladies on board?'

TWO

The St Vincent

JOHN STARED INTO HIS HALF EMPTY MUG as if he were trying to discern his distant youth in the trembling reflection.

'I never intended to go to sea', he began.

'Life back then was different. Growing up in Tipperary as the third son left me with few choices. I'm sure you'd understand that situation completely! For a time I did seriously consider joining the Church: but which one? We Catholics were, shall we say, not the most popular people with the establishment and changing religion just to secure a job would have broken my mother's heart. Then there was the other problem: that most Catholic priests had to go off and study in France.

'I suppose, truth be told, that I was a little spoilt by my mother and sulked at the idea of leaving home.

-"I know how you feel" I interjected wryly.

John grunted, a warm smile filling his features, and then continued his story. 'In my own defence, it was quite understandable. Remember, I grew up cocooned in a very privileged family and was totally unaware that ninety nine percent of my countrymen were struggling just to exist.

'You're acquainted with the history of the Scully family? So you'd know the legend of my grandfather James and how it overshadowed all of the Scullys during our growing up. Grandfather James was a great business man! My father used to say that Granda had two guiding principles in his life. The first was to create wealth and the second one was to protect it! Perhaps that's one of the reasons why I was so spoiled.

'By the time my father took over running the bank, I was living in a grand house with several servants and I had my own tutor. So it's not difficult to see that my understanding of life was blinkered to say the least. Believe me, I can honestly say that I had a great childhood, so why risk it all by heading off to a cold cloister in France?

"At least you were given a choice" I said.

'From what you tell me it sounds like you used up all your choices Frankie. But as you'd well know, being a pampered child makes one an expert in prevarication and I was a veritable prodigy at putting off any decision. Looking back I think my father understood that. By then my tutor had reached the limits of his capabilities, and he'd also fallen in love. The promise of a new life in New York and his desire to get married helped precipitate what happened next. I seem to remember him telling me that he was going to head for America. "There's no scope here in Ireland for anyone who likes to think for himself, John", he said, and he was probably right. My father didn't want me lounging around at home under his feet, so it was off to Dublin for me to continue my education.

'Back then it wasn't too hard for someone with money and half a brain to get into Trinity, so *quod erat demonstrandum*, I became a Trinity student for a time. I was only sixteen and very wet behind the ears.

'I was too young to join in with student life there, even if I'd wanted to – which I didn't – so those first few months were some of the loneliest in my life. Don't get me wrong, Dublin's a great city for the craic, getting drunk, getting into fights and going to church to confess your sins. It was great fun seeing the older lads with their hangovers on a Saturday morning and me as fresh as a daisy.' My uncle let out a soft chuckle, and took a sip of his rummy tea.

'But for whatever reason, student life at Trinity didn't seem to be leading me anywhere so I moved on to the Kings Inn in the Easter term of 1829. The idea was for me to learn the law and maybe even go on and study for the bar. Failing that, there was always politics. The family owned a few boroughs in Ireland, so finding a seat in Parliament wouldn't have been too hard. In fact, later on my younger brother Francis went that road and he's turned into a fine man. He was the one who bailed me out when the Tipperary Bank went bust and we lost us all our inheritance. But that didn't happen until much later, some years after I'd returned from Australia.

'Having grown up living a carefree life in rural Tipperary left me with mixed feelings about Kings Inn, which I found too stuffy for my way of thinking. I wanted to spread my wings. My old tutor's talk of America had planted an itchy idea in my mind and I needed to scratch it. It got to the point that even dear ol' dirty Dublin was losing its lustre, yet I didn't have a clue as to what I would do. I just couldn't seem to make a decision to save my own life.

'Finally my father made the decision for me. "It's the army for you, my lad", he informed me when I turned twenty-one. "I've bought you a commission in the 80th foot. It's a sound regiment. The garrison is up in Dublin so you won't be far from home." And that was it. I was to be a lieutenant to guard and protect His Majesty's people in dear old Ireland.

'From then on the army became my new family and the security of army life really suited me. It wasn't just the security of army life, it was exactly what I needed to help me grow up and take on some responsibility for my life. I was however, what my sergeant major would describe as a 'big eejit' and totally ignorant of how quickly things can change in the army.

'We'd all just settled in at Dublin castle when orders arrived informing us that we were to take over guard duty for the convict ships destined for the penal colony in New South Wales. Most of us had never even heard of the place and when we discovered that Australia was on the other side of the world, it seemed that our careers were destined to be spent in exile.

"You never thought of going to America" I asked.

'Once you're in the army you don't get any options. The powers that be in the British army weren't concerned about what I wanted or that I barely knew their rules or regulations, and they were even less interested in the fact that I'd only just come to grips with living away from home. The orders that I received meant that I faced the imminent prospect of heading off to the antipodes and the chance of never setting foot in Ireland again.

'The commission that my father had purchased meant that as an officer in His Majesty's army I had to do as I was ordered, which made me wonder whether he'd had any fore-knowledge of our assignment.

"Now that sounds familiar" I said.

'Our designated ship was the *St Vincent*, normally a cargo vessel. It had been fitted out to take two hundred convicts, more or less, and it was usually more, between decks. She was due to leave Cork in early September in order to miss the wild spring storms that have sunk many a ship south of the equator. That gave us just two months to relocate our troop south, prepare the ship and receive the prisoners for transport. There was a great deal to do, which perversely, and yet thankfully, didn't leave us much time to think about our own situations.

'We travelled down to Cork in fine summer weather with the countryside looking glorious and green. The sun was so hot that we had to unbutton our coats to cool down. It makes me laugh now to think that we thought we were hot in an Irish summer. One summer in New South Wales taught us what real heat was, and you had to do more than just unbutton your coat to cool down in that part of the world!

'But on our march south the locals were out picking berries from hedgerows, and cocks of hay were appearing in the fields. The farmers in the Pale were having a grand summer and harvest promised to be one of the best. Further to the west I'd heard from the family that things weren't looking quite as good. I'd also heard, but not from the family, that there was a deal of unrest in that quarter.

"I remember Pa telling us about those times. That must have been just before the Great Famine. A lot of Irish headed to America around then." Just talking about that awful period in Irish history made us both quiet. "Sorry John. Do carry on, I'm fascinated by your story."

'Well, we made good time and arrived in Cork about the same time as a column of prisoners was marching into town under the watchful eyes of guards. The ragtag collection of manacled humans were ordered to wait whilst we marched past. Each and every one of us felt their stares as we filed past them. "There but for the grace of God go I", one of my men whispered to me, and it was a fact that many of our own rank and file could easily have ended up being with those wretches if they hadn't taken the Kings Shilling, and they had been hated for doing so. As I looked at those destitute souls with their chained limbs, I determined that I should take good care of my men because they'd made a very brave choice.

'Our billet was to be on board the *St Vincent*, so we made straight for the harbour. Having made such good time we surprised the master of the ship, one Captain Muddle, who seemed rather contrary at the extra burden caused by our presence. "Muddle by name, muddle by nature." That's what Donald Stewart used to say. He was in charge of the 3rd East Kent Regiment of Foot popularly known as "the Buffs", though I never did work out why they called them that.

"Not sure that I'd like to be in that outfit." The rum was bringing out the wittier side of my mind. John, quite rightly, ignored me.

'Donald was a good ten years older than me, but he was a decent fellow, if a little soft. His brother had a much senior rank than he did and I think he felt a bit overawed by the whole military thing. Donald had sailed from Deptford in England on August 8, 1836, and had done a fair job in getting things straight on board. I got to know him well on the trip, as you would do when you spend most of your spare time in a nine-by-nine-foot room. But even if we had a choice, there was no point complaining. At least our cabin was at the rear of the ship and well away from the prison deck.

'All in all, things went fairly smoothly in those first few days and at least the captain seemed to know what he was about so we muddled our way through, if you'll forgive the pun!

"Another sip of rum Frankie, just to keep the damp out of your bones." I gratefully accepted his offer, then watched as he put another shovel of coal on the fire. John settled back into his chair and continued talking.

'Out in the harbour of Cork were two hulks, the holding pens for our co-transportees to the new world. To a young man's eyes, they looked to be terrible places. Big, old, floating coffin ships emasculated of their masts and standing off alone like the pariahs they were.

'We took a lighter over to the *Surprise* and went on board. The smell was the first thing to hit you. The foul vapours emanating from below deck would knock you over they were so putrid. I cannot imagine what hellish atmosphere would evolve if the two sets of prisoners assigned to the large leather bellows at either end of that decrepit wreck ever stopped pumping clean air into the prisoners section!

'We inquired after the health of the prisoners and were told that Surgeon Henderson had made his inspection on the previous day and found them all to be fit for the journey. Surgeon Henderson's reputation went before him, having sailed with several convict ships in years past. From the little that I knew of the man, I didn't relish spending too much time in his company!

'Taking one of my men with me, I went below. Our consignment of convicts was held in cages and secured with leg chains as a precaution. There had been no information of any prison break and I doubt that any of those poor creatures had the strength to knock the froth off a pint of beer, but these were unsettled times and all precautions had to be taken.

'When my head ducked under the lintel allowing me my first view of the prisoners quarters, I was struck by how clean it was despite the awful smell. "It's all the piss and shit what 'as soaked into the timbers an' not even the Pope 'isself could exorcise that stink", a cheerful guard from the Buffs informed me. All the prisoners wore the clothes they'd arrived in, which created a motley picture against the dull background. However, my Buff attendant informed me, with perhaps just a little too much enthusiasm in his voice, that before embarkation onto the *St Vincent*, each convict would be stripped and scrubbed till their skin bled. He went on to tell me that their heads would be shaved and finally that they'd be given their convicts clothes: jackets and waistcoats of blue cloth, duck trousers, coarse linen shirts, yarn stockings and a wooden hat. "Mind you, if the weather turns a'fore yers leave, they won't 'arf feel the cold", he added, rubbing his hands and slapping his thighs in glee. The soldier was a disagreeable sort and I'm happy to say that I never saw him again.

"Kinda makes me doubly glad I never was in the buffs." John rolled his eyes towards heaven in mock exasperation's the my weak humour.

'Each day since their arrival, the prisoners had been allowed on deck for exercise whilst a detail of other prisoners swabbed out the empty cage. Outside each of those barred cages was a small ledge where a butt of water was kept, refreshed by a "trusty" from amongst the younger, incarcerated lads.

"'They look a fairly healthy lot", I mentioned to my Buff acquaintance.

"'It's summer, ain't it", he replied, a little downcast. But, perking up, he added with relish, "You should see the sods we take on board at the end of winter though, 'alf starved they is!" A part of me hopes to God that he was forced to retire early with a bad dose of the gout!

'Returning to the deck, I sucked in great lungsful of the clean salt air and shaded my eyes from the bright grey light of a Cork autumn day. Gulls circled overhead, squawking and swooping in the hope of scraps. We left the hulk and returned to the *St Vincent*. There I began to learn the ropes about life on board the ship that was to be our floating home for the next four months.

'Thankfully, the *St Vincent* was only ten years old. She'd been built in Deptford, which meant that she'd be solid and well-constructed. I'd heard many a gruesome story about some of the older ships that'd sailed to New South Wales and very few of them filled me with any delight. Contractors were finishing off the ship's fit-out, which had been begun in Deptford, so by now it was fully ready to receive its cargo of humanity. A sailmaker was busy making and repairing the final hammocks for my men as well as for the convicts, although many of the latter would have to share timber bunks. These seven foot by seven foot squares of misery would accommodate three prisoners each.

'According to Surgeon Henderson, that was the ideal way for lice to travel from one human to another. As if to test my intestinal fortitude, he went on to inform me that it was also why some of the more vulnerable amongst the prisoners were sodomised by the most depraved amongst their brutal companions.

"What's that" I exclaimed. Life on the plains had protected me from some of the harsher realities of life. Life in Dublin soon changed all that though. John chose not to answer me but continued with his saga.

'Looking back down the years, it was a terrible thing for a young man to assume such a huge responsibility. I was so very much out of my depth after my sheltered early life. But then again, it may have been a blessing, because if I'd known what I was about to endure, then the life of a curate in France may have seemed more attractive after all.

'Getting used to life in such confined spaces takes a great deal of adaptation as the occasions for conflict are great and many. Donald was the senior rank amongst us, but he seemed a reluctant leader at best.

'Then there was Captain Muddle, who was in charge of the ship's crew and the general running of the ship. This was his second run to New South Wales, but it had been ten years since the last one. He freely admitted that he was only doing it for the money seeing as there wasn't much else on offer at present. According to the local tittle tattle, he needed to get away from home for a bit, although he didn't explain that last reason himself.

'Surgeon Henderson was an old hand, having completed a few convict runs already. He was a man of fixed ideas but at heart I believe that he had the best of intentions towards the prisoners, it was just the rest of us that he disdained!

'But the little man with the biggest power, at least in port, was the Naval Agent. I never knew his name, everyone called him the little man, but only behind his back because he was a powerful bully. Mind you, he had reason to be. The process of fitting out and supplying ships leaving for the other side of the world created opportunities for those less honest operators who were ever ready to exploit the system. For all his faults, the little man saw to it that the fit-out in Deptford was spot-on, and if a barrel came up light on the scales then there was hell to pay. By the look of his nose, he'd fought a few fights to prove his point and I never met anyone who was willing to take him on – even Surgeon Henderson was polite to him.'

THREE

Setting sail

'WE WOKE ON THE MORNING OF 12 SEPTEM-
ber knowing that on the morrow we'd be hoisting the Blue
Peter and heading off to the Southern Hemisphere. It was in
those last twenty-four hours that a vast amount of work still
remained to be done.

'The previous day one of the prisoners from the *Surprise*
had been transferred across early. Dominic Doherty was
twenty going on fifty. According to the guard of the *Surprise*,
he'd slipped during morning exercise and broken his wrist,
although during my later conversations with Dom when he
was working for McLeod up at Patrick Plains in New South
Wales, he indicated that he may have been on the receiving
end of some rough treatment by the guards.

'Surgeon Henderson had seen him and splinted the arm. The
good doctor believed that the bones would knit well, meaning
that Dom would be fit to travel. As a precaution though, he'd
been ordered to transfer across early just in case there were
any further mishaps, as each convict had to be accounted for.

John paused in his conversation and smiled to himself at a
memory that had just surfaced from the distant past.

'There was one other prisoner who was sent across as well but at the time none of us were really sure why. It was only later that we learned the embarrassing truth. John Murphy was a Cork man who had a yen for women of easy virtue. One of the uncomfortable consequences of, how should I put it, intercourse with those ladies of the night was that the male member can suffer as a consequence. Fortunately John had the sort of character which meant he wore such misfortunes as a badge of honour. "I couldn't pee", he told me with a knowing wink. "The ol' fella blew up like a balloon and just dripped like the village pump. And mi' pride and joy was covered with little cauliflowers, 'cept I doubt you'd want to eat them."

'For a moment I thought he might actually show me his "pride and joy" but he went on, a little crest-fallen. "But the good doctor's put paid to my gallop for now. Sliced my little beauty right up the middle and be-dad it made my eyes water when he did that. After that I could piss as far as England!" and he spat over the side in the general direction of His Majesty's homeland!

'As he recovered from his painful circumcision, he claimed that his newly acquired gait was a result of coming from a long line of nautical men and that it was in his blood to walk like that! John managed to milk six weeks on the sick list before he returned to life between decks.

'The morning before our departure was the day set apart to take on our supplies, and what a store it was. I remember it as if it were yesterday. I must have checked the list a thousand times, perhaps that's why I can remember every last detail of it. We took on 12,828 pounds of bread in 104 bags; 2,655 pounds of tobacco in six puncheons, six hogsheads, and two small casks with forty-eight iron hoops. All of this was to supplement that which had been taken on in Deptford. Thus John began his long list of items but I soon lost interest after the forty-eight iron hoops. I must have yawned because he took the hint saying 'Sorry laddie, you and Maria have more in common than meets the eye!' With that he continued on with the story of his voyage.

'Finally we were fully stocked and the ship stood a full foot lower in the water. All we needed now was for our convicts and our passengers to join us and we were ready to set sail on the morrow. The weather was holding for early September and we faced a clean exit from the harbor. But first we needed a good night's sleep before the long journey into the unknown would begin. Believe you me, I slept like the dead that night!

'The ship's mate rang the bell at dawn, causing us all to tumble from our bunks and dress quick smart for duty. Within minutes the ship was alive with bustle and shouts. To the casual observer one would think they were watching a dance in a madhouse, such were the comings and goings. Yet every person who dodged and weaved past the other knew what he was about and where he was headed.

'The first to come aboard were the wives and children who were to accompany us – six women and seven children who appeared terrified of the ordeal they were about to undertake. Then the free settlers came up the gangway, the ten sons of convicts who'd served their time in New South Wales. They stayed a close bunch for most of the trip, unsure as to whether they were part of us or part of them. Generally speaking, they were good lads and helped us with provisioning the prisoners and keeping water up to them when the weather got hot near the equator.

'But one poor mite, John Healy, looked a half-starved creature. In fact, it only took a couple of days of sailing before he ended up in the care of Surgeon Henderson, although that may have not suited him the best. Our good doctor decided that the lad was constipated and fed him copious amounts of castor oil to get him "moving". I'm not sure if it was the castor oil or the better rations which he received, but over the next two weeks the lad seemed to grow in front of our eyes.

'Finally the hulks disgorged their contents. First up was the *Elsen*. She was to provide 120 new souls for the great southern land. They sat on the benches in the longboat holding their chains in their laps. The transfer was going smoothly enough when suddenly the third boat was caught by a freak wave and one prisoner found his leg trapped between the gunwale of the tender and the side of the *St Vincent*. His scream was piercing, causing all to run to the rail to see what had happened. Another prisoner who went to his aid became unbalanced and fell overboard and sank swiftly, weighed down by his iron chains. One of the crew jumped into the water and for many moments we thought he had drowned too. Then the surface erupted and a great shout went up as he held the poor convict's head above the water until they were gaffed and dragged to safety.

'Surgeon Henderson arrived on the scene and summed it up swiftly. The victim with the crushed leg was deemed unfit for passage. He instructed the guards to place the poor fellow to one side to await repatriation and almost certainly, the surgeon's saw to remove his crushed leg. The other man was brought up unconscious. He had a vicious wound on his forehead which Henderson rapidly attended to. Smelling salts were tried to no avail and the man remained motionless. "Send him back", was all the surgeon said before returning to his cabin. The other convicts filed past the two men as they lay on the deck unsure whether to feel pity or jealousy.

'The prisoners had been issued numbers when they entered the hulk and now each group of them was assigned a cage below decks. As they descended the stairs and reached their cages, the blacksmith was there to knock their leg chains off and release them into what were to be their homes for the next 120 days.

'Over the ensuing hours, the *Elsen* and the *Surprise* released their contents and then we shut them up again in the *St Vincent*. Guards were posted. Meanwhile the passengers had lined up on the deck, the free settlers crowding together in a small group near the gangway, trying to gain one last glimpse of any family who had come to say goodbye. I searched the small crowds hoping to see a familiar face but could see none. I turned to head to my cabin and almost bumped into my father!

'He said it was one of the perks of buying a commission for one's son: and that was the reason he'd been allowed on board to say goodbye. We shook hands and for one of the few times in my life, words failed me. As I stared into his face I became aware of someone standing behind him and when I glanced in that direction I saw it was my mother.

'I realise that it's not good form to cry in front of your men, or anyone in fact, but I must admit that I had tears in my eyes as we clasped each other close. I can't remember her exact words as she was sobbing away herself, but in essence she told me she loved me and to take care of myself amongst all those savages. For my part, I promised to write as often as I could, although I had no idea how often any ships would be carrying mail back from that part of the world. Then the final bell rang and all non-passengers had to disembark.

'You know, there are episodes in your life that seem to go on forever and yet when you try to remember them, the details are blurred. But those few minutes with my parents are as vivid to me now as they were then. I can still see my father's cravat with its diamond pin in the middle, the lavender scent that my mother used all her life and the pressure of my father's hand when he finally bade me farewell. I never saw him alive again.'

'That sounds a lot different to my leaving home John. Pa left me at the rail head, then got in his buggy and left. Though, you know what?' I didn't wait for him to answer, 'I'd really like to be certain that I'll see him again.' I looked at my empty mug and smiled 'Must be the rum making me nostalgic in my old age.'

'Don't be too hard on your father Frankie' was all John said on that subject.

'So then the gangplank was drawn up, the foresail canvas dropped and most on board said goodbye to Ireland forever.

'We were towed out into the mainstream of the harbour and Captain Muddle began the job of getting his vessel underway. The 80th and the Buffs were well organised and we had little to do for the rest of the day. As we sailed out beyond sight of our old home, our thoughts turned to surviving the long voyage, and wondering what it would bring us.'

FOUR

The way to a mans heart.

JOHN WAS ABOUT TO TELL ME ABOUT HIS
voyage when there was a rattling at the front door and a heavy
foot could be heard entering the hallway. 'I'm home, John.' The
happy voice of Maria Scully bounced along the walls and into
the kitchen. John hurriedly pushed the bottle of rum toward
me. From his frantic signalling, I knew that I should hide it
about my person. There was the sound of a heavy coat being
removed and shaken outside the still-open front door – I could
tell it was still open because of the freezing draught that was
now embracing my legs.

The door slammed shut, caught by an errant gust of wind,
and the brass dolphin jumped in surprise. Maria sailed into
the kitchen and we men rose to greet her. 'My dear, this is
Francis Scully, William's lad from Minnesota.'

'Kansas', I corrected him. 'Very pleased to meet you, Mrs
Scully. It's very good of you to take me in', I said, holding out
my hand in anticipation.

'Do they grow them all this strapping big in America?' she
teased. 'Come on now Frankie, give your old aunt a decent hug.'
She held her arms wide and I sank into her generous bosom. The

embrace caused a flutter of sherry and rosewater to confuse my senses but her flushed face suggested that she and her lady friends had enjoyed a very convivial afternoon together. 'I see that John made you a cup of tea in them auld mugs that aren't fit for the cat.' Over her shoulder I spotted the man of the house roll his eyes toward heaven. 'Ah well, old dogs and new tricks, eh Frankie?' and she gave me a conspiratorial wink that I was to become very familiar with in the months ahead.

'Has the good man asked if you had a mouth on you?' Maria inquired. Seeing the look on my face she went on, 'Ah well, leopards and spots, eh Frankie. But sit ye down and I'll see if we can find something to feed a growing man, eh?' With that she picked up her pinafore and began to bustle around the kitchen. She fired out random questions as she collected her tools of trade, a frying pan and a big white loaf of bread. 'Do they have sausages in America?' she asked over her shoulder but before I could answer she finished. 'Well I doubt they're as fine as Irish ones, eh?'

John rose to his feet, cleared his throat and said, 'Perhaps it would be better if Frankie and I got out from under your feet and went into the parlour, my dear.'

'That's a grand idea, John. You do that and make sure you build up the fire. It's starting to get bitterly cold out there.' She nodded her head in the general direction of the kitchen window.

'You may as well bring your tea with you if it's not cold, Frankie', he said, and twitched his head in the direction of the door with a knowing look. I picked up the cold mug and followed him along the narrow passageway and into the front parlour. He headed straight over to the small bookshelf.

From behind a collection of the works of Charles Dickens, he produced yet another half bottle of rum. He held it up to the light. 'Looks like there's still a couple of noggins in it', he said benignly whilst tilting the neck of the bottle in the direction of my tea cup.

I settled into my chair while John stoked and poked the fire. He opened the newspaper and held it in front of the fire. 'It helps draw the flames', he explained but before I could ask why, the centre of the paper suddenly ignited and sucked the whole flaming sheet up the chimney. 'Best close the door', he said sheepishly. 'This house is dreadful for the draughts.'

With the fire now glittering with flames, the rum heating our stomachs and flushing our faces, John took up his tale of the *St Vincent* once again.

FIVE

Voyage to New South Wales

'AS WE PICKED UP THE WIND AND ADJUSTED our sails for a southerly course, my friend Dom from the Buffs nailed the sailing orders to the door of our tiny cabin on the rear deck.

SHIP'S STANDING ORDERS

8 o'clock: Piper to sound for breakfast, and again at 12 o'clock for dinner.

The grog always to be served at 1 o'clock and at half past 4 in the evening.

The people never to be disturbed at these meals if possible.

No clothes to be hung up to dry in the rigging, but ropes to be kept for that purpose fore and aft between the fore and main masts.

No naked light under any circumstances to be taken into a store room.

The Warrant Officers are never to convert or expend any stores, not even a nail, without first obtaining consent of the duty Officer.

The ship's company and soldiers are to be mustered at Quarters every evening at sunset and everything ready for action to prevent being surprised in the night.

The watches at sea to be mustered – sailors by the officers and soldiers by the sergeants. The sergeant to report to the officer of the watch any absentees.

'I smiled at Dom saying that if everything was going to be as easy as nailing orders to the back of a door, then we should be in for a very pleasant voyage.

'All things being equal, we had enough stores to see us all the way to New South Wales without having to stop. But being at the mercy of the weather on such a long voyage, anything could happen. Thanks be to God the wind gods were kind to us and before the steady pull of a strong southerly we were able to unfurl the main sails and make good time. The biggest challenge we had in that first week under canvas was to find our sea legs. It's a peculiarity of the Irish people that although our little island is surrounded by water, not many of us are good sailors – apart from St Brendan that is! It took me two days before I stopped feeding the fish, but once I got used to the hawing and lurching of the *St Vincent*, I came to love a life at sea, cosseted by the ship's timbers.

'We didn't see too many other sails as we crossed the Bay of Biscay, but on the seventh day we saw white sails on our starboard quarter bearing down on us. The captain held his course and made signal for her to declare herself. She raised an American flag. We could now clearly see that she was a brig and she sent a signal to see if there was a surgeon on board. Captain Muddle replied in the affirmative, gave orders for the jolly boat to be lowered and requested that Surgeon Henderson join our detachment of guards.

'We came alongside the brig and climbed up on board. It was a sight that haunts me even today. She was a Portuguese slave ship with close on 600 women on board bound for Rio de Janeiro. The master of the ship proudly told us that whenever any of the slaves had shown any signs of illness, he'd thrown them overboard to prevent others coming down with the contagion. So far, in their journey from Benguela in Africa, over fifty of those poor souls had perished. And the reason for his request to see a surgeon? He was suffering from the gout as a result of too much strong wine!

'On our way back to the *St Vincent*, not much was said but all out hearts were affected by what we'd seen.'

That's awful John. I just can't imagine ..." and words failed me.

"I know. The world was changing but when it came to slavery, it wasn't changing half fast enough."

'On the *St Vincent*, the condition of our own transportees seemed to improve as we headed south. For many of them, this was the first time they'd had regular meals for most of their short lives. When I compared the lives that they'd lived with mine, my conscience was pricked with a sensation that I can only describe as humility.

'But soldiers don't have time for emotions; they are paid to obey orders. Each morning when the piper sounded the alert, I looked at the notice pinned on the rear of our door and was amazed at how well we'd actually kept to it. Then things changed.

'In many ways Dom was not a strong man and perhaps a calling into the Protestant Church would have suited him better. Army life just didn't. It was the wrong fit, if you follow me, so it came as no great surprise when he fell sick with a sore throat. For the first few days we dismissed it as a winter chill.

But one night he woke me to say he felt like he was almost choking to death and by the next morning he couldn't even swallow his own saliva. That's when we began to think that it might be a bit more serious.

'I tapped on Surgeon Henderson's cabin door, which was next to ours on the rear deck. He asked me to hold the lantern and told Dom to open his mouth. The poor man was in so much pain it was almost impossible to obey the surgeon. But Henderson was not a man to cross and soon had poor Dom opening as wide as he was able. I could see the beads of perspiration running down his cheeks and yet the man was shivering like a child coming in from making a snowman.

"'It's the Quinsy', said Henderson in a rapid fire voice. "Easy to fix. Just have to lance it and let the pus out. You'll feel much better after that."

'The look on poor Dom's face was a study in abject fear. If he wasn't as white as a sheet before he'd seen the doc's scalpel, he surely was afterwards. He looked at me with pleading eyes, begging me to do something. I asked the good surgeon whether there might just possibly be some alternative to pushing a sharp blade into my friends throat, and was met with an icy, "No".

'He got Dom to sit in a chair and positioned me with my lantern so that he could get the best possible view. "Want to hit the right spot. Can't afford to miss, eh?" His words were less than reassuring to my now frantic friend. At the sight of the blade, Dom fainted. "Good", commented Henderson. "Makes it much easier. Hold the light closer there."

'He put a sort of gag in his patient's mouth. It operated like a small rabbit snare, except in reverse. By pressing a lever the blades forced the jaw wider so that even I could see the malignant bulge at the back of the throat. Using a long sharp blade, he pierced the most glistening part and immediately a stream of pale pus exuded from the fresh wound. I'd expected a foul smell to accompany the corruption but none came. As if reading my mind, Henderson said, "Doesn't usually smell. Worse if it does. He'll be fine."

'With unexpected gentleness, Henderson used a clean gauze square to squeeze the quinsy and remove as much pus as he could from Dom's mouth. "Don't want to spoil his breakfast, do we."That was the closest I ever heard the man make to an attempt at humour in all the time I knew him.

'He passed me some smelling salts which I administered with almost magical effect. My friend roused himself from his stupor with a mixture of pure relief and agony at the residual pain in his gorge. "Sick list for two weeks. More work for you, eh Lieutenant Scully?"With that, Henderson dismissed us back to our cabin.

'Dom's recovery was slow, which meant that I was officer on call day and night for the next few weeks. It seemed such a big responsibility at the time, and yet looking back it was one of the best things that could have happened to me. Up until that stage I'd been just a junior officer who'd managed to avoid all attention, thereby hoping not to make any mistakes. Now, when something went wrong, it was up to me to not only deal with the situation, but to accept responsibility for it. Overall, that extra burden of command made me a better officer. What I had feared actually made me stronger. Sound familiar?

"Not yet" I replied, "but I have a strange feeling that all that's about to change."

'The routine pinned to the back of our small cabin door became tattered and ignored because it had become ingrained in our lives. Things on board went surprisingly smoothly, and even Surgeon Henderson became bored. "Obstipatis", he said to me one meal time. I excused myself for my ignorance of the condition before he halted me, pointed his fork in my direction and explained, "Can't shit. Bunged up to the eyeballs. Castor oil. Running out of the damned stuff." He relieved his fork of its burden before picking up a glass of claret and downing it in one. "Didn't train to be a surgeon to shovel shit." Pushing his chair back, he pulled out his pipe, filled it with tobacco and fell silent for the rest of the meal, fogging the dining room with clouds of pungent smoke.

'The one recurring friction we did have on board was not with the convicts, although they could give as good as they were given verbally. It came with the aggravation between the guards and the crew. Our lads had nice uniforms, which I suppose gave the sailors to believe that they were the superior creatures. The crew baited my men about being little more than nursemaids. Being only young men, you could understand why it wounded their manly pride. On three occasions fights broke out, resulting in me having to order one of my own men, a man named Goss, to receive fifteen lashes.

'Captain Muddle found himself in a similar position. For his part, he'd ordered many a lashing and didn't bat an eyelid. For a young officer like me, I felt every lash as if it were on my own skin. Later, when I went to see Corporal Goss after he'd been seen by Surgeon Henderson, he grinned wryly and said, "I deserved it, Surr. I caught him a fair belt in the gob and that made the pain all the sweeter." He even held out his hand and said, "No harm done, Surr. Let bygones be bygones." I met him some years later and he never uttered one word about that lashing. He was a fine man and I was led to understand that in later years he was a great man in his community. Sometimes a good tongue lashing is more painful that a real one!'

My uncle paused, and as if on cue, a voice pierced the darkness that had now inhabited the hallway: 'Yer food's on the table, lads. Come and get it whilst it's still hot.'

SIX

Life in Anglesea Road

AUNT MARIA WAS RIGHT. IRISH SAUSAGES were much better than American ones. Not that I had had much experience of those tasty tubular monsters, sausages not being a big part of life out on the plains of Kansas.

Those evening meals were to become typical of life under the Scullys' semidetached roof. We sat around the kitchen table with its blue, chequered oil cloth. In the middle was a wooden cutting board proudly displaying the latest towering, black-crusted invention of Culley the baker. 'The best pan in the whole of Dublin', Maria would declare cheerfully, layering it with a thick coating of butter that left the impression of her teeth in its bitten edges.

I soon came to realise that for Maria and John, mealtime was a silent affair. I suppose that after twenty-five years of marriage, and not having any children of their own to discuss or worry about, they had little to talk about anymore. Both were clinical in their attachment to their faith yet did not appear to be particularly passionate about it. Grace was said before each meal and I obliged by joining in the ritual. Maria was quick to note my perfunctory approach to prayer. 'Do they have any churches in your part of the world, Frankie?' she asked archly with the plump end of a pork sausage about to disappear into her mouth.

'They sure do Maria', I gleefully replied. 'There's one about 150 miles away. We get to go visit there every few months. It's kinda cute and there's always a crowd of people there when you go. I remember as a kid that after Mass we used to get the best lemonade that I ever did taste.' Looking up, I noticed that perhaps their liking for lemonade wasn't as great as mine was.

'So you don't get to the sacraments that often then, eh?' John broke in.

'I'm not too sure I understand what you mean.'

'Confession and receiving Holy Communion', he added, sounding a little superior and yet miffed at the same time.

'Oh yes', I lied. 'Whenever I can I take that host. Pa insists upon it.' I finished, trying to sound serious. In fact, Pa didn't have much faith in the Catholic religion. 'It sucks the vitals out of a man, if you ask me', was his pithy summation of 1,900 years of the Catholic faith.

'Have you left many broken hearts behind you, Frankie?' Maria asked, prodding her fork into yet another juicy sausage and winking outrageously at me.

'Oh no, Mame.' It was an interesting fact, I found, that lying in Ireland seemed as easy to do as it did in the US. 'Anyways, the nearest girls to our farm are fifteen miles away.' One of the reasons I'd been sent overseas to Ireland was because of my predilection for the local girls! My father's reasoning being that an Irish girl would never behave like American girls do.

'So is it the Kings Inn that you'll be going to?' It was John's turn to continue the interrogation. 'I went there for a short time before I got my commission', he said as he buttered himself a thick slice of bread. 'Didn't suit', he added, 'the study of law is a dry ole thing for most young men'. I looked at Maria but she seemed more interested in selecting her third sausage than in anything her husband was saying.

'I'm afraid not, John.' I finished my mouthful before speaking. 'Trinity. The fees have been paid and term begins next week, I believe.'

'That's grand. I'll walk you in and show you around, and if we have time I'll show you a few other delights Dublin has to offer. Now finish up your food. It's a sin to waste any, and Ireland just out of an odious famine.' Although he spoke the words in a light tone, his expression seemed haunted by the very mention of the word 'famine'. Even Maria paused and looked across at him as if sharing some awful secret.

What with all the travel and the rum, and even though I was sleeping in a strange house in a strange bed in a very strange country, that night I slept like an Indian.

I was roused by the sound of John descending the stairs. It was to be the first time I heard that well-known rendition of 'Footsteps on an Irish staircase', or 'The slippered foot on the squeaking step'. In my room it was still very dark, there being no street illumination at the rear of the house. The small fire was long cold and so was everything else in the room. I got out of bed and immediately regretted it. That cosy little bedroom had turned into an icebox overnight. I reached for my longjohns, my vests, my trousers, my socks and anything that might hold in some shred of heat. I fell back on the bed hopping into my socks and eventually my body began to warm.

I recreated John's symphony on the stairs and found him in the kitchen with the lamp lit and the kettle heating on the hob. 'What time is it, John?' I inquired, trying to tame my unruly hair.

'The church clock just rang a quarter to eight. I'm fixing some tea for Maria. Would you like some?'

'Anything, as long as it's hot" I said, blowing warm air into my cupped hands and moving closer to the range.

'Ay', John said smiling. 'It's a bit fresh this morning, but then, that's dear old Ireland for you, raining one day, raining the next and everything damp and cold inside and out all the time.' He pulled an extra mug down from the shelf and placed a frypan on the hot plate. 'There's a few of them sausages left over that will do us for breakfast. Maria won't be down for a bit. She likes a lie in on these mornings.' There was no malice in the way he said it, but I thought there was a bit of sadness in his voice as if he was missing something. 'After that we'll put on some warm coats and head off into town, if you're up to it.'

'Sounds fine by me', I replied, and listened to the sound of the sausage skin begin to sizzle as the heat did its job.

The walk along Merrion Road and into the city didn't take long. As we got closer, the crowds became more plentiful. I saw building styles that I had never seen before, apart from the brief period I had stayed in New York waiting for my ship to sail. These mansions were three storeys high and gave the impression of casting a most imperial gaze on us lesser folk as we strolled by. Small squares opened up with bare trees standing like sentries guarding the barren grass patches beneath. In summer, I thought, they would be great places to sit and enjoy the sunshine. As if reading my thoughts, John remarked, 'They're grand little squares in summer. It's a shame that we don't often get the weather to enjoy them.'

'What's that building there at the end of the park, John?' I pointed to what appeared to be the front of a Greek or Roman temple.

'That old place, young lad, is the Royal College of Surgeons. Some mighty grand gentlemen have come out of that establishment. I believe that some of them even went to your part of the world and taught them a thing or two.'

'Any chance that I'd be able to visit there sometime?'

'Certainly, my lad. I just so happen to know one or two people who work there.' A twinkle appeared in his rheumy eye. 'You know why the emblem of Ireland is the harp, don't you?'

It was plainly obvious that I had no notion of what he was getting at so I simply replied, 'No'.

'Well, you see, it's not what you know, but which strings you need to pull to find out!' He smiled at his own humour and then led me down along Grafton Street toward the River Liffey. At that early hour of the morning, it seemed quite idyllic leaning on the bridge parapet and staring into the waters below. 'It's not a place you'd want to be wandering about on your own after dark', John warned me. Even at that early hour there were already a few gurriers lurking in darkened alleyways, their pinched faces eyeing off likely targets for their crimes.

The Liffey itself was a patriotic colour of green. My idyllic musings were shattered when I saw a dead dog float past under the bridge. Looking further along the banks, I saw old furniture and debris stuck in the mud and the slimed walls of the embankment shrouded the scene with a deeply depressing atmosphere.

'Let's get a coffee in the Gresham', John volunteered. 'It's down the other end of Sackville Street. We'll see how it stacks up against the stuff they give you in America.' We headed up the wide boulevard past impressive shop fronts with the towering figure of Nelson looking down on us from his perch in the middle of the street.

That was the first of many walks that John and I had around Dublin. For all its dirtiness and the threat of impending thievery, there was something about the city that was intoxicating and addictive. In the beginning I had great difficulty even understanding what the Dubliners were saying, their accent being so different from Uncle John's. But I loved their wit, I loved the way they could sing together, fight with each other, get drunk with each other and then turn up like polished penitents at the weekly Sunday Mass. They were the most honest hypocrites I had ever encountered.

Maria loved the theatre and her Sundays with the ladies. John disliked the theatre and loved a quiet Sunday at home reading by the fire. The outcome was that when Maria had no escort, it became my delight to accompany her to all the theatres and playhouses around Dublin, and sometimes beyond. On those other Sundays I sat with John and listened as he talked, or if the weather was fine, the two of us would walk down to Dún Laoghaire pier to look out over the harbour whilst the gulls wheeled and screamed overhead, diving down for the odd chip thrown to them by tourists and other Sunday promenaders.

'Flying rats', John muttered. 'They're the same all around the world. Scavengers! They look so pure and white but anything is game for them, half-living or dead. Mind you, they're not the only ones. Down on the Swan River they have birds which the locals call magpies, except they're not. Too big. My friend Drummond there told me their proper name is a butcherbird. Doesn't matter what name you call them, they'd peck the eyes out of a newborn lamb, and I've seen them knock a dove out of the air and then a mob of them eat the poor thing alive! Bastards!'

'So I take it that you're not a great fan of birds then, John', I interjected, trying to brighten the mood.

'Birds, is it?' he replied. 'No, birds, I like birds and I really admire the big raptors like the wedge-tailed eagle or the sparrowhawks. They're majestic killers. The others are just scavengers. Why can't they stick to worms or other things that crawl under rocks?' He was on the verge of slipping into a black mood when he seemed to take a grip on his senses and lift them back into the light.

'Talking of rocks, have I told you about the rocks at the entrance to the harbour in New South Wales?'

Sensing the arrival of a good story, I happily replied,

'Not yet

SEVEN

New South Wales

'BELIEVE ME, TRAVELLING TO NEW SOUTH Wales used to take an awful long time. It took us 116 days to sail from Cork to Port Phillip. A few days out from port, one of the sailors said to me, "Enjoy the grey skies whilst you can Lieutenant because once you get to Sydney town, you'll soon get sick of blue skies." Being an Irishman, that sounded really funny, but after having lived down under for several years I completely understand what he was talking about. That midday sun can burn the skin off you, especially if you have blue eyes, fair skin and freckles.

'But the sea I didn't mind. Vast open spaces of grey blue as far as the eye could see. After growing up in dear old Ireland where the grey skies seem to press down on you day after grey day, that vast ocean of blueness was a balm to my eyes.

We saw flying fish and marvelled at the dolphins as they leapt in front of our prow. We even saw some whales blowing, but they were some way off. They're leviathans! They just swim around with their big gobs open trawling up tiny little fish. When they've had enough, they just doze off on the surface without a worry in the world – apart from us humans that is.

I've heard tell of ships being sunk when they accidentally ran into one of these sleeping monsters.

'But we didn't see any mermaids. Mind you, that was probably a good thing with so many men on board just itching for female company. There were a few fights when the talk turned to women, but there's nothing like a dozen lashes to cool a man's ardour and bring him back to his senses.

'Having so much time on our hands left plenty of time for reading and such. I'd write my journal, but wondered if anyone would ever bother to read it, including myself. I wrote some letters to my mother and father, but after a few weeks there was such little news to record that I stopped completely. I'd taken the precaution of packing some books as well as the bible. Mr Dickens's *Pickwick Papers* had just been published and for a colonial Irishman, I found them to be very amusing and mightily informative. I'd never realised how much things were changing over there in England. I thought it was just we Irish who seemed to have a mortgage on all the troubles in the world. Mind you, there was one common thread which united both countries: Catholics were definitely second class citizens on both sides of the Irish Sea.

'The more I read and the more I reflected, the more I developed an itch that I couldn't rightly scratch. It was the feeling of a great moral discomfort at being a gaoler. And not just any gaoler, but a gaoler to men whose major crime had been to steal in order to survive. These men weren't that much different to people like myself, except that they hadn't been born a banker's son. They'd stolen to stay alive. Lads like the Murphys. John stole a coat and Ted stole a sheep and they both got seven years transportation. And young Francie Madden, he was only a scut of an errand boy from Drogheda, for goodness sake.

The lad was 15, they caught him stealing clothes to keep him warm and he gets seven years too. Mind you there were some real villains amongst them who deserved to be locked away and the key thrown in the deepest part of the ocean.

'But most of them are a blur to me now. I do remember poor John Chambers though. He had a funny accent and made the lads laugh with the strange way he spoke. Birmingham is where he grew up and where he signed up for the army, too. It turned out that he didn't suit the army and army life didn't suit him either, so he deserted. He thought he'd be fine in Kilkenny, of all places. Naturally, with a Birmingham accent, he got found out and was sentenced to seven years. I heard tell later that he'd started making a life for himself working his sentence up on the Paterson River, but a snake bit him and he died. I wonder will anyone else ever remember him.

'By the time we came in view of the lighthouse on the South Heads everyone knew everyone else. A sudden summer squall swept in from the north and we had to head back out to sea to avoid being swept into those towering cliffs on either side of the great estuary that leads into Port Phillip Bay. After two days of very uncomfortable living within sight of our destination, the wind dropped away and the sun came out. We fired our cannon and were answered by the lookout on the cliff top. Raising our colours, we entered the heads and sailed into that magnificent bay.

'It's massive and took us a good three hours to reach the dockside. That gave us all time to study our new home. To our eyes everything looked familiar and yet very different. The wooded areas seemed as green as back home. The settlement had a church steeple and as we came closer we could clearly see the Hyde Park Barracks where our prisoners were to be taken.

'But as the tiny buildings became bigger and bigger, and as the trees became individuals and not vast swathes of wooded land, we became aware that this was no new Ireland or England or even Wales. Even the air smelled different. It was so clean and so fresh with just the hint of eucalyptus coming off those strange trees around the expanding settlement. But port life is port life wherever you are in the world, and it was no different to back home, except of course for the weather.

'It was so hot and so humid! The lads were lined up on the deck in full regalia and soon began to sweat like pigs beneath their thick, woollen uniform coats. A couple of them even fainted but that was probably because of the double rum ration that they'd been issued with earlier. Down on the wharf a company from the barracks was dockside to greet us. The detachment's captain came on board as soon as we were tied up. We handed over the papers and gave our reports over to him as per Her Majesty's regulations. Surgeon Henderson reported of the only death we'd experienced and in a most out-of-character jest even suggested that the poor man may have died of boredom as there was so little to do.

'The company were given shore leave. A guard was left on board, more for disciplinary reasons than for any concern about safety for the ship. Sydney was a young, exciting and expanding metropolis with tens of thousands of souls living in a cauldron of convicts, soldiers and free settlers. It lifted my heart to see so few convicts in chains; even our own men were led away unfettered. Sad to say though, for some of them, that wouldn't last long. For the recidivists, the chains were clapped back on again when they broke their bonds and it was "back to prison for you, boyo". But the first thing I learned on disembarking was the great Australian salute! And let me tell you, it had nothing to do with military protocol.

'It's to do with the flies – the flies there are unbelievable! They come at you in their millions. These lads are not the scaredy cat ones we have here in Ireland where if you swat at one, that's usually the end of the affair. These Australian ones are a different breed altogether! They descend on you in vast clouds, invading every orifice exposed to their inquisitiveness, and they stick to you closer than a bad smell. They say that in the bush you can tell if someone is near, because your cloud of flies suddenly gets even bigger. Everyone there is constantly waving them off and that's why they call it the Australian salute. If it weren't so miserable it would be funny but after a day marching with flies feeding off our sweat, I can tell you, not many of us Irish lads were laughing much. The only things to equal them in nuisance value – apart from the ants, the spiders and the heat – are the mosquitoes. They are the ultimate, demonic destroyers of a decent night's sleep.

'Walking through the streets of Sydney was a real eye-opener. I'd come from Tipperary where there was a definite hierarchy to life. Our family had survived and prospered in the Irish part of Great Britain by learning to adapt. We'd made our money by being the middle men between the landholders and the tenant farmers. It's not an easy job, believe you me, being a middleman. Most seem to think that being a land agent is all about having to kowtow to the landed gentry, but in fact in most of those gentlemen don't want to have anything to do with running farms. Most of them prefer to live the high life in London rather than in the damp, wild west of rural Ireland. Not all of them, mind. Some are the finest people you'd ever meet in a month of Sundays. No, the hardest part about being an agent in Ireland is to look in the eyes of the tenant farmer who hasn't got a brass farthing to his name and ask him for his long overdue rent. There's no doubt that can be the cruellest part of the game.

'The funny thing is that some of those poor wretches are just as conniving as some of their landlords. Most just want live in peace and quiet, and make enough to feed their families and have a bit to put aside after the crops or cattle are sold. But they can be a canny lot too! When it suits them, they know how to pull the wool over your eyes. I can remember many a story of my father's where a tenant would swear on his mother's grave that his sheep had died of the scour and they couldn't afford the rent, when he knew for a certainty that they'd moved them to a cousin's place in another townland. It's a time-honoured game in most cases. But it's one of those games where you'd like to think that all sides can save face and feel that they've won. The genius of a good land agent is to know how to negotiate that middle path. That's how we Scullys lived for generations until Grandfather decided to branch out into the banking business.

'I've lost the thread of what I was talking about. Now where was I? Ah yes, walking down the main street of Sydney.

'There were shops, small businesses and a whole hive of activity everywhere. They weren't owned by convicts and they certainly weren't all owned by ex-military men, either. Most of them were owned and run very successfully by second generation Australians, the children of convicts who'd worked their sentences and won their freedom. These young businessmen had no fear of the government and felt under no obligation to those in charge. They had a wonderful confidence in themselves, as if liberated from the web spun by the British for so many centuries. They knew the law and they knew they were needed by the government to generate income for the state coffers, and boy, were they were making the most of it!

'For a young Irishman who'd only known British ways and British customs, such freedom caused a heady confusion.

'I found a licensed premises and went in to taste my first beer on Australian soil. I'm not sure what caused the greater surprise, the fact that the beer was shipped over from England or that the landlord was … how shall I say … a somewhat theatrical character. His name was David and whenever I was in Sydney during my time in New South Wales, I always made a point of calling in to see him. Despite his somewhat effete manner, David was the genuine article once you had become used to his startling physiognomy. He was a huge, fat lump of a man with a large dewlap swinging below his receding chin. His hair stood up on end in a totally unmanageable fashion and his face was constantly beaded with perspiration, winter as well as summer. Yet he was honest and generous and absorbed the drunken slurs of his customers like water off a duck's back.

'"Don't mind them, Lieutenant", he would say. "In the morning when they're sober, they won't remember what they said, so why should I worry about it? And some of them are my best customers", he would add, giving me a knowing wink. Later on I was to discover that away from his gin palace he lived in a splendid house in a suburb called Surrey Hills. Whenever he invited me there he would show me something new, saying, "Look what my customers bought for me this week, Lieutenant", indicating some new painting or ornate piece of furniture of exquisite taste.

'For a landlord, David was an interesting man because he didn't drink beer and he didn't drink wine either. "But I do love rum", he would say with that cheeky sparkle in his eyes. It was soon apparent that it was the rum that caused his face to bead in perspiration, and not just the humid summer weather of Sydney town. He kept his own bottle of the brown liquid behind the bar, and worked his way through it during the course of the day. Yet despite his weakness for rum he was a kind man who was always good to me. In fact, it was he who gave me snippets of news about another place I was to call home for many years, the Swan River Settlement.

"'That's the place for a young man with vision", he told me. "Apparently there's hardly anyone there and there are no convicts – we don't like our boys in chains, do we?" he added, giving me a knowing nudge. "I also hear rumours that the potential for grazing sheep is huge, and what with all the wars in Europe...' His eyes opened wide as theatre orbs and the flesh under his chin fairly trembled with excitement as he spoke the words. Picking up a small tumbler of his favourite tipple, he added, "I'll keep you posted on any news I get. You never know, we might just end up in business together", and he would laugh the laugh of a truly liberated human being.

'The prisoners were held in the Hyde Park Barracks next to the newly built cathedral. Catholic emancipation had reached Sydney the year before in the shape of Governor Bourke, who was coming to the end of his term. In many peoples' eyes, he had performed a great service by making all religions equal in the colony and removing the Anglican Church as the establishment church. Needless to say, that didn't happen without considerable feeling from people on both side of that religious fence!

'The Catholic bishop in Sydney at the time was an Englishman named Polding, a good man who served his people well.

He was a breath of fresh air and cut from a different cloth than those pretentious prelates back in Ireland who wanted everyone to fall on their knees and kiss their rings! Old Polding was a true Benedictine, but he knew how to fight for his flock if his people were threatened. He used to hold meetings in the old chapel, next to the new cathedral, and every man and his dog had time to say their piece and expect to be heard, but that didn't mean that he'd agree with what was said. At one of those meetings he was informed that one of the Supreme Court judges, a man called Willis, had proclaimed to his Anglican confreres that the Catholics were nothing but idolaters! Well, the old man fired up like a rocket!!

"'Let me tell you a few truths about the Doctrine of the Eucharist that appear to have been missed by our most *esteemed* Judge Willis", he declared sarcastically, before announcing to one and all that he was off to see Governor Gipps to give him a piece of his mind! If it hadn't been for the intervention of several senior gentleman – including the attorney- general – then holy war might have ensued. You have to remember that even back in England, Catholics had only just been allowed to practise their own faith and there were still an awful lot of people in London who thought of us as a band of thugs just waiting to overthrow the king!

'Increasingly, the clergy who were arriving down under weren't English. They'd trained in places like France and Italy, and Father McEnroe had even been Vicar General in America, so we knew we were connected to a much bigger world than England and her empire.

'In that sense, it took some time for dear old Bishop Polding to understand that Australia was a child of the world. I think he had the idea that he could tame the wild colonials with a decent, English Benedictine education. It was a grand vision and I'm sure that if we'd had a few more monasteries and fewer public houses then it wouldn't have done any harm at all.

'But the poor man was up against it. Most of the convicts and free settlers were Paddies escaping from dear old Ireland after the potato failed and famine loomed. And of course that meant a lot of exiled Irish priests came out to care for their countrymen and they didn't take to kindly to the English yoke … *again*! No, dear old Bishop Polding had to abandon his monastic dream and accept the Irish influence. I still wonder though, what the place would look like now if he'd persevered. Yet those priests weren't just bog-Irish and stupid. Father Geoghegan studied in Spain and Father Brady had spent ten years running La Reunion, which if you don't know is a large island off Africa where French is the native language!

'Strangely enough, most of the inmates of the Hyde Park Barracks next door to the cathedral were Catholics, and Irish ones at that too! There were usually about 600 prisoners held there at any one time. Mr Backhouse, who was one of those evangelical men, described it as a "rather handsome brick building"! It might be handsome on the outside, but inside there were more than a few black-hearted people, in and out of uniform.

'It's a mighty place though. At the front it's three storeys high, and behind that a central open area surrounded on the other three sides by single storeyed buildings. At each corner are circular domed structures which look more like overgrown bee hives; that's where the guards keep an eye on their customers twenty-four hours a day.

'The front entrance is designed to intimidate. It's a massive edifice decked out with great Greek columns and faux Greek sculptures. Enter its hallowed portal and you'll find yourself in the nerve centre of the place where all the planning and assignments are worked out. Above that, on the next two levels, are the wards holding the prisoners before they're allocated their assignments. Most of them weren't there for long, which was a good thing because they were packed in like sardines, their hammocks slung in single tiers from one side of the room to the other. Yet despite the cramped conditions, the rooms were clean and airy. The biggest challenge was to keep the newcomers away from those evil dregs of society which the system seems to strain and filter into such institutions.

'The lads with useful trades like carpenters or smithies were put in a separate ward, and so were the poor creatures who were awaiting their various punishments. Back then, flogging was the punishment of choice and some of the poor devils were beaten until their flesh was almost hanging off. Fair due to him, Bourke put a stop to that. He put a limit on how much a man could take. Mind you, fifty lashes would probably have half killed me. I wouldn't be far off the mark if I said that upward of a thousand people were being flogged each year when I first arrived, yet according to the officer in charge at the time, he was of the opinion that even though the prisoners dreaded it, they felt "degraded" if they hadn't been flogged. And once they'd been flogged it was as if they'd joined the floggers club and they became quite reckless about the whole thing. Human nature is a mighty deep mystery, young man, and the mind of a young man is an even deeper mystery!

'Hyde Park was not the only barracks around at the time. There was Carter's Barracks which was to be found a bit further south of the main settlement. It was generally used as a debtors prison but it had a chain gang too. It was right next door to the treadmill which, I suppose, was a handy place to keep their minds and bodies occupied. Then there was the old goal. That was where the condemned were held. The mere thought of it makes me shiver! The less said about that place the better. And last, but not least, that great British invention, the hulks in the harbour. You'd have to wonder what sort of black mind came up with the idea of taking the prisoners from one hulk on one side of the world to then lock them up in another hulk on the other side of the world.

'Whoever came up with the term "civil servant"?'

EIGHT

I have my eyes opened

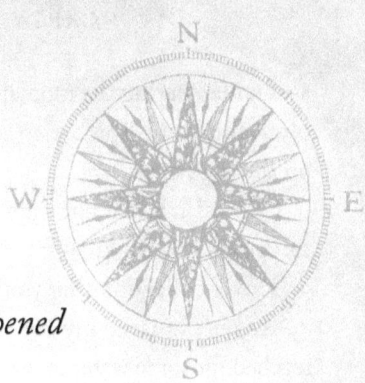

I'D BEEN SITTING FOR SOME TIME LISTEN-
ing to my uncle. The two of us were in a small cafe near Dún
Laoghaire, which boasted a great view over the harbour. Well,
it would have been a great view if the wind hadn't been driving
the rain against the windows, blurring the view with a million
orbs which raced and chased each other down the panes in
stop-start cascades.

The tea pot had been placed over a small candle. John
reached for the pot and offered me a second cup.

'More tea?' he asked. Foolishly, I agreed and a thick brown
liquid oozed out of the spout and into my cup.

'How can you drink this stuff' I asked him. 'Mind you', I
continued, 'it's better than your coffee which is like …' and
here words failed me.

John smiled one of his relaxed smiles, the sort that made his
old eyes twinkle. 'It's funny, you know', he replied, 'the little
habits and idiosyncrasies we take for granted on a daily basis
and which we never really stop to question. Remind me to
tell you what a Spanish monk told me when he found himself
lost, and he and his brothers had run out of water.' He paused

as if remembering the moment vividly. 'You know Frankie, we often think our lives are so tough, but in reality we're living on the pig's back.'

I sipped my tea, not quite sure whether that was a good thing or a bad thing.

'How's college suiting you?' he asked.

'It's not.' I placed my cup back on its fine china saucer and reached for some water to wash the foul taste of tea dregs from my mouth. 'It's just so dry, John. And the law just doesn't seem to go anywhere. All it seems to do is head off down various dead ends until you run out of precedents and that's it. And it seems so cruel too, unless you've got a bucketload of money and then who cares, really? If you're lucky enough to be ridiculously rich, you just keep paying your lawyer until the other side runs out of money or the courts run out of time. Then you carry on with your life as if nothing has happened. But if you steal a chicken to feed your family then it's "string him up" or transportation for life!'

'You're a very earnest young man, Frankie', John said quietly. 'And I respect you for that. I was like that too and it almost killed me.' He picked up his cup, drained the last drop and placed it down again, rattling both cup and saucer as he did so. 'Come on, we'd better get back otherwise we'll have worse than the law to deal with.'

We headed home under his big black umbrella, our brogue shoes splashing the puddles caused by the late autumn showers.

Looking back, I remember these times with John with great tenderness. He was the first male to treat me as an equal, to listen to what I had to say and not lecture me on what I should be thinking or doing. Even from the other side of the Atlantic Ocean, Pa still managed to rile me with his monthly letter demanding to know how I was progressing and what the political climate was like in Ireland. All the man seemed to want to do was to get richer and more powerful. I have to admit, he made me even more determined to make the most of not having to live under his shadow. Now here I was living in Dublin and enjoying my first real taste of freedom. But giving a young men his unfettered freedom will often lead him down a rabbit hole of mediocre memories. I have to admit that my enthusiasm for studying evaporated shortly after the Christmas vacation.

Christmas: now that's a great time to be in Dublin with parties and pubs staying open late nearly every day of the week. Christmas Day itself was almost a bit of a relief from all the partying. That's if you discount the mountain of food that Maria had prepared for the three of us. But at least my intake of porter and whiskey was diminished for a couple of days, and that couldn't be a bad thing!

'How's the study going?' Maria asked, passing me what appeared to be the thigh of a small ostrich to supplement my already-overladen plate.

I glanced quickly at John, who gave me a sly wink. 'Grand, Aunt', I replied, and stuffed another Brussels sprout into my mouth, which had the double effect of ceasing conversation and making my aunt very happy. When John and I had filled ourselves to the point of bursting, Maria finally relented and allowed us to retire to the front parlour. 'I'll bring in a few mince pies to fill in the corners in a little while', she said with a beatific smile, satisfied at a job well done. "Feeding her men", as she called it. 'And John', she shouted down the corridor. 'Give the lad a glass of port to drive out the winter chills. The poor lad isn't used to our Dublin Christmases. We don't want him freezing to death now, do we?'

From the size of the glasses John served the port in, I came to the conclusion that he might be expecting a second Ice Age!

'Sláinte', he said, and we both took a deep draught of the dry, amber liquid. It had the almost instantaneous effect of warming the heart and making the pain in my stomach easier to tolerate.

'Great stuff, John', I commented. 'Sure as hell tastes a lot better than some of the stuff I've drunk in Kansas!' I beamed happily at him. John nursed his glass and looked into it as if trying to decipher some hidden message deep within its golden glow. He looked up at me.

'You know Frankie, sometimes I forget that whilst we Irish were struggling to survive the Great Famine and emigration, and the Australians were struggling to put down roots in that unforgiving country on the other side of the world, you Yankees were doing your damnedest to wipe each other off the face of the planet!' He sipped on his port and gave me a searching look. 'Tell me lad, what was it like growing up during the war over there? Did it affect you and the family much?'

We Americans can be pretty full of ourselves and in most cases we have a great deal of things that we can be mighty proud of. But the Civil War would have to be the blackest mark on our country's history since mankind first stepped foot on that great and glorious land. I pray to God that it'll never be repeated until the end of all times. Uncle John's question caught me by surprise. Running my finger around the edge of my glass, I looked deep into it. My mind was momentarily mesmerised by the traces of alcohol as they stretched their 'legs' up the sides of the glass.

'We didn't see much of what happened back then, John, although we weren't that far from the Confederate border. Everyone in our small town was affected by it though. Most lost a brother or a father, an uncle or a cousin. Some lost them all. There was a deal of grieving back then and a lot of graves to attend to.' Christmas suddenly felt a long way away. 'Then they shot Abe Lincoln. That one shot killed a great man and wounded a whole nation. We're still coming to terms with it all.'

John sat there watching silently as the light faded from the leaden sky outside.

'Pa took it worse than I expected. It's a funny thing, whenever one of Mr Lincoln's speeches appeared in the paper, Pa'd almost go red in the face reading it. He thought the man was plain mad. He reckoned Mr Lincoln was hell bent on ruining the country and destroying all the opportunities that America offered to people such as himself. Then the President gets shot and Pa is devastated. He didn't talk to anyone for a whole day! Ma tried her best but then she was pretty shook up, too. I was just a little sprat so I just out and asked what was upsetting him. He looked at me in a way he'd never done before, and has never done since and said, "They just killed our youth."'

Maria bustled in with a tray of mince pies liberally sprinkled with icing sugar. 'Ye are all very serious lookin", she lilted jollily. 'These little dainties should put the heart back into you.' She placed the tray on a small table and handed each of us a small plate. 'Now don't be shy Frankie. Don't be going back to America as thin as a rake and them blaming me for not feeding you up enough. Come on, John', she rounded on her relaxed spouse. 'Pour the young lad a another drink, it's Christmas after all. Maybe later on we'll go for a little stroll just to help our meal go down, before we have some sandwiches, eh?' The grimace on John's face was reflected by the groan in my stomach.

'Is this trial by ordeal, Maria? Or will you give the lad a break?' John took the smallest pie he could find and placed it on his plate to please his wife.

'He's a growing lad and needs his food', she said, smiling back at him and crossing her arms across her ample chest. 'And while you're at it, you'd better put some more coal on that fire, there's going to be a frost tonight if this cloud clears and my old bones are right.' Dusting herself down, she turned and left, closing the door behind her.

'She's a sound woman', John said in a masterful sort of way, 'and like all good women she loves to feed her men to death!' He picked up the coal shuttle and tipped the black coal on the fire. Immediately the room felt colder and a plume of grey smoke filled the grate before heading up the chimney. 'That's the trouble with coal fires on a damp day like today. You get just as much smoke going into the room as you get heat going up the chimney!'

'Back home', I mused, after a pause and seeing the small flickering flames finger the edges of the coals, 'we'd burn big wood fires because it can turn pretty cold over there. At night the pond out back would freeze over and so would the water in the rainwater butt. But when I think of Christmas, I think of that big open fire with the wood spitting on the floor and the smell of the maple logs burning and shifting in the grate. I remember my Ma, too, even though she died when I was still just a little guy. She always used to let me sit on her lap in front of the fire and she'd hum tunes from way back.' All those memories seemed to surface in a rush and John respected them all with the silence that he allowed to embrace us both.

NINE

Slavery

THINKING BACK ON IT, I WAS DRUNK. BE-lieving myself to have the mind of Rousseau and the oratorical skills of Abe Lincoln, I launched into a slurred speech, the words of which have shamed me ever since. 'You know what, John, where I come from, if you lock people up, put them in chains, condemn them to treadmills and then give them the lash if they step out of line, we call that slavery.' I nestled back into my chair feeling smug at my blinding insights!

I saw a flash of anger in the old man's eyes – the first and only time I ever saw it.

'You Americans only gave up slavery when you were financially comfortable enough to gripe about it, young man. One hundred years ago you were happy enough for England to send you convicts to work your fields and build your railway lines so that your founding fathers could grow fat off their labours!' Each time he said 'your', he spat the word at me.

There was a bustling in the corridor and Maria arrived in the room. 'That's the trouble with Irishmen. Leave them alone with a bottle without the calming influence of a good woman and they're bound to start a fight! What is this one about?

Politics? Religion?' She looked at the two of us in turn. 'Cat got your tongues?' She pulled her apron up over her head and folded it slowly and neatly before saying, 'I'm just going to put the kettle on so if you can keep from each other's throats until I get back, I'd much appreciate it.'

'Sorry', mumbled John, and I added my own humbled apology too.

When the door had shut and the sound of quiet had settled in our minds, John said, 'We're talking about forty years ago Frankie, and even though it sounds trite, it was a different world back then. If you settle for a moment then perhaps I can do a bit of explaining about it all.' My journey from stupidity to sobriety had taken all of ten seconds. I pushed my glass away from me and listened to my uncle.

TEN

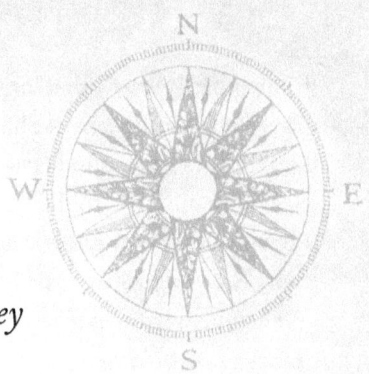

Politics and money

'WE ALL THOUGHT WE WERE DOING OUR duty and obeying rules. Rules that were meant to improve the lives of the English, the Irish and even the Americans, by sending those convicts out to New South Wales. We were taking the so-called dregs of society to the other side of the world so that the good people of England and Ireland could live in peace. Well, that's how the theory went. But in the end it was all about money!

'The original idea for transportation – firstly, I may add, to America –was to save money on building new prisons in England. For a country that was constantly at war with someone or other on the Continent, money was scarce and every penny had to be saved. The idea of exporting one problem from one place to provide cheap labour in another must have seemed like a very attractive proposition at the time. But then your Yankee rebellion came along and England lost America, and you Americans lost the taste for English convicts. Which, by the way, I whole-heartedly agree with.

'But that still left dear old Mother England with the problem of what to do with her rising prison population.

Remember, it wasn't that long before your American tragedy played out that Britain was having her own troubles in Crimea as well, not to mention Persia, India, China and South Africa. And with all those soldiers and walking wounded returning home, you'll never guess what happened, shock and horror, there were no jobs to come back to, and little prospect of one either. The outcome: a great deal of those soldiers ended up in places like Newgate Prison. That foul place was meant to hold 500 prisoners, but; as far as I know the number never fell below 800.

'So some mighty genius came up with the idea of the Hulks. Big old ships lying in the Thames crowded with the overflow from the prisons. They weren't the most hygienic of places, but then neither were the prisons. Did you know that a couple of prisoners were taken from Newgate to the Old Bailey for trial? The only trouble was that no-one knew that they had typhus! The upshot of that was that the judge of that venerable institution upped and died, and so did the jury, and even the lawyers got what some thought were their just desserts, too. In fact, about fifty people in all died from that dose of typhus, and what a mighty uproar it caused at the time, but only because it affected the gentrified classes.

'All this unsanitary stuff led to a great discussion about prison and penal reform. By then Botany Bay was in full swing with prisoners being sent out and being used to help settlers develop the land. But the bigwigs back in London thought that they were having any easy time of it, "wandering the countryside without a care in the world". Hadn't they been sent out there as a punishment? Shouldn't they be getting re-formed instead of rewarded? And even amongst the free settlers in the colony, there were those who muttered about the terrible influence of "all these evil people" in our town. All these pressures squeezed the governors to find solutions to keep everyone happy.

'Meanwhile, out in the colony, settlers were crying out for help to work the land. The colony's executive wanted more roads built and more housing created, but the big bosses back in London were saying, "You're spending too much money", and, "The convicts should be better secured in the penal settlement and you can't keep spending money on them."

Governor Darling tried to bring some order to it all but one of the problems he had was that the boyos in the army were worse than the villains they were supposed to be guarding. And to make matters worse, although Darling believed in reform, he didn't think much of the men he was supposed to be reforming! Do you know what he called the transportees? "Double distilled villains." Ah Frankie, you have to love a verbose, aristocratic Englishman when he's in full flight!

'We have a deal of those windbags back in the States as well. We call them Congressmen' I interjected. John smiled.

'Funny how things don't always work out the way the legislators would like them to though, eh? When Governor Burke came along, he could see that making convicts suffer greater and longer punishments after they'd arrived would in fact be counter-productive. What he actually said was, "Five years of slavery will be more likely to impede than promote reformation."

'Burke was a man of his times. He was very devout and believed in raising the moral well-being of his convicts. He didn't allow gambling or bartering of any kind, and he punished anyone who used foul language. He allowed the regulation dispensation of grog but over and above that he abhorred drunkenness. Then on Sundays the superintendent was to muster all the men and read prayers to them. He even made sure that the peace was kept during the rest of the day so that the men could read the Good Book. How's that for a bit of enlightenment?

'He was a bit of a stickler for quantifying things, even the types of punishment the prisoners received. So, for a first offence you'd get fifty lashes. After that, if you offended again, the number went up to 100 lashes. It sounds inhuman now, but for those times it was quite an improvement! In fact, when you look at his time in office, and see the level of reform he enacted, you'd have to say that Governor Bourke was a real force for good for just about everyone in New South Wales.

'All of these shenanigans were going on at a time when road building itself was adapting to the new scientific and industrial age. New principles to do with adequate drainage, the cutting of culverts to reduce the steepness of a road's descent, and putting a camber on a road so that the water drained away adequately were all being introduced to road construction. In order for that to happen, proper engineers had to be employed to oversee it all. So now the hierarchy of a work party became an engineer or his assistant building a road, in charge of an iron gang of sixty men with an overseer – usually a ticket-of-leave man acting as the go-between.'

'What the heck is a ticket of leave man?'

'I think in your part of the world you'd describe it as being out on parole.

'And they did all this in the remotest part of the colony! You could see why there was a great potential for disaster, or, at best, things not working out as planned!

'I learned all this from my short stay at headquarters but had no idea where I, or my detachment, would fit in.

'I didn't have to wait long to find out!'

ELEVEN

On the road

'OUR ORDERS WERE TO PROCEED TO THE garrison at Windsor, way out along the Western Road. This was the same track that farmers drove their sheep and cattle back into Sydney along to be slaughtered down near the Harbour Rocks. And it was the same track that the labourers, the military, assorted tradespeople, prisoners, ticket-of-leave men and peripatetic preachers set out to find work, and help those struggling souls already scratching a living out in the often unforgiving bush.

'Despite the humid weather and the constant threat of thunderstorms, the dust from the road rose up and choked us. It didn't help that my head was still a little thick after the previous evening's excess at David's public house, and I had frequent recourse to the supply wagon to refill my flask with fresh water – a rare commodity the further you moved away from that fledgling city. It made me smile to think that lack of water could ever be a problem back in dear old Ireland. But then just about everything about this country of New South Wales was different to the land I'd left behind.

'Sydney town was as different from Dublin as chalk is from cheese. Don't get me wrong, there were some impressive brick and sandstone buildings. Take St Mary's Cathedral for instance. Now that grand building could match it with the best churches in Ireland and England. At the other end of the building scale things were a lot different as most dwelling houses were built of wood. As for the roads, none were sealed once you got too far away from Sydney itself, so in summer you breathed in great gobfuls of dust, and in winter you were mired in mud.

'The trees down there are so very different, too. I thought them to be the most straggly things that ever had the temerity to call themselves a tree. Even the leaves rattled! Most of the trees we came across were eucalypts which none of us had seen before. They've got long slender leaves coated with a waxy surface and drop rock hard nuts that pool along the roadsides, washed there by the seasonal downpours of rain. Those nuts are a constant threat to man and beast with their unstable surfaces and yet a cockatoo will sit in the branches and crack those nuts in their beaks as easy as if they were eating cheese

As a source for shade on a hot summers day, eucalypts are hopeless, but by God, they're mighty fine trees when it comes to producing wood! It's as hard as granite and many's the nail I've bent trying to drive into it. And heavy ... I've seen a cart crushed to smithereens when just one branch of those trees fell on it. And it burns as hot as coal in a fire.

'Talking of which, everyone who lives there has a great respect for fires. You wouldn't want to be starting a fire outside in summer in that part of the world. One spark and ten thousand acres can go up in smoke and once one of those bushfires gets going there's no man on this earth that can stop it.

Prayer is the only answer. Praying to the good Lord Almighty that the wind changes or the heavens open. Thank God I've only experienced a few fires but the devastation they produce is unbelievable. Everything is destroyed – trees, bush, cattle, wild beasts, everything except the bloody flies!

'Even the grass is different in the colony. Well, they call it grass. Just sitting on it can be an act of courage or foolishness, that's if you can find any at all. It's so spiky that it's enough to drive a man mad with the constant irritation it causes to the flesh.

'But the irritation doesn't stop there. The ants are so big that one lady at a picnic told the new curate that the one just about to climb up his trouser leg was big enough to run errands. And they can have a ferocious bite too, the ants that is, not the curates! Them bull ants make most outdoor entertaining a sort of survival of the fittest. Many's the new trooper who has been unknowingly sat down on one of their nests – and believe you me, they never make the same mistake again! Most locals stay standing with a wary eye on the ground around their feet, or tuck their trousers into their socks. It's a habit we all picked up very quickly!

'It sounds a pretty crazy place John! Why do the folk stay there if it's so inhospitable?'

'Once you get to look beyond the scary stories and see the real beauty that's there, you begin to see what a great country it is. And it's not just the fauna, the flora or the climate that was the greatest revelation for me. It was the native blacks. They seem different in so many respects. They look like the Negro but have straight black hair, and their faces are different, too. For a start, they've got a flattened ridge across their nose and they're not as tall as the African Negro. Their children are pure delight! They seem so full of innocent fun with their big brown eyes and strangely enough, some of them actually have blond hair. I would hazard a guess that they must be some of the happiest children on this earth.

'The adult black is different though. They rarely look you in the face, mainly because they're a naturally shy people, but those who've left the bush and moved into the towns have taken up the worst of British habits. They gather together to get drunk in dry creek beds, fighting and shouting at each other in a most pitiful way.

'I suppose it's like a lot of the stories I've heard about the natives in America. The majority of the Aboriginal blacks are grand people. They pick things up faster than you'd think and seem to be the equal to of any man I know. It took me a long time to learn a few words of their language, but they appear to learn English easily, and the women are very nimble with their hands. Yet for some mysterious reason, the opinion of the establishment was that they're very lazy fellows and make unreliable workers.

'Once we'd left the settlement behind, I quickly realised that in the bush everything is a work in progress. Thankfully, some of the gentlemen in charge in Sydney there were pretty smart people who were planning the expansion of the colony with great foresight. They'd used some of that wisdom to provide wells along the expanding major routes so that the more distant areas could be better served.

'The cattle didn't seem to worry too much about the weather, and had learned to shelter under trees during the hottest parts of the day. Those not-so-dumb creatures never strayed far from the dams that local farmers had dug ... with the help of convict labour of course. The convicts weren't too dumb either!

They're pretty fond of sheltering under any shade trees they can find in the heat of the day, and fair enough. Out there in the bush there aren't too many landowners or supervisors who'd thrash their workers for not working in that broiling heat, even if they could've mustered the strength to do it. But woe betide any convict who was dumb enough to not have his ticket-of-leave with him.

'I heard tell of a man called Grape who was found on the road. In those days anyone could be stopped and asked to identify themselves. If they didn't have their pass, then there could be hell to pay. Well, this man Grape told the policeman that he was a freeman. His story was that he'd been working for an ex-army man who ran a big farm nearby. It turned out that the army man was a brute with the whip and our man Grape had had enough of his lashings and decided to run away. Unfortunately for poor Mr Grape, all he had in his pockets were a couple of pieces of lead which he claimed he needed to write with – but strangely enough, he had no paper to write on.

'Well, the local magistrate decided to find out who this Grape person was, so he sent him down to Sydney where there are very senior government gentlemen who are experts in telling people who they are and where they belong. It turned out that these noble individuals decided that our Mr Grape was still a convict, and just to prove the point they sent him off to Norfolk Island to cool his heels for a few years! The poor fool had run away from one frying pan only to jump straight into a terrible fire!

'Do you know what happened to him afterwards?'

'No.' The word seemed to have a terrible finality about it. After a pause, John carried on with his story.

'We followed the Western Road until we came to the Great Dividing Range and from there we headed north for a short way until we reached our HQ at Windsor. The barracks weren't that much older than the road having been built in the early '20s, and were comfortable enough for our needs. There was room for fifty soldiers, and at another barracks room for up to 100 convicts. It was easy to tell the difference between the two: ours had a wooden stockade around it, and theirs had a high brick wall!

'For better or worse, it proved to be a brief stay, as the army's orders were that we were to be split up and sent to smaller outposts around the countryside. But, for the time being, this was to be our home and it felt good not to be on the move for a few weeks.

'Windsor's a decent, small, but bustling little town with four schools, three churches and thirteen pubs.: a bit like Ireland really! As well as that there was the goal, a courthouse and stores, too. All in all, Windsor was a hive of activity and home to nearly 1,200 souls. Our job was not only to help keep the peace and protect the settlers from hostile natives, but also to help the farmers when labour was in short supply, especially at harvest time. But in January and February all anyone wanted to do was to stay out of the sun and wait for the cooler weather.

'Once we'd billeted the men, I went to report to Major James Nunn, our commanding officer. My first impressions were not good, but mind you, neither were any of the subsequent ones. He was an arrogant man, typical of the supercilious class that give all officers a bad name. He greeted me officially and then told me that I was to take a squad of convicts the following morning to clear debris away from the foundations of the bridge over the dried-up river. "Give you a feel for the place", he said, and then dismissed me. No welcome, no, "how was your trip?" The man had the charm of cold rice pudding!

'Being a Tipperary man, I'd been reared to respect those in charge. But coming from a family of land agents, I was also accustomed to dealing with the Major Nunns of the world. But as they say, first impressions are lasting.

'Within days, we settled into usual army routine. Orders were given and orders were carried out; soldiers marched here, soldiers marched there. Convicts were counted and taken out in work gangs, convicts were counted and then brought home again. Normally, there's little time left to socialise.

'I was just getting used to our new routine when, one day in March of 1837, Major Nunn called me into his office and, without any adieu, handed me a piece of paper. I took it from him and read the letter that declared that I'd been promoted to captain and was to take charge of the stockade at Hassan's Wall out on the Western Road. I must admit that a smug smile crept onto my face. Major Nunn looked up.

'"Something funny, Mr Scully?" he asked without a smidgeon of happiness on his face.

'"No, Sir", I replied, handing him back the paper as he returned to writing entries in his logbook.

'Without looking up he continued, "You're to report to Hassan's Wall and take charge there. You'll be overseeing the ironed gangs working on the bridges. Been a bit of trouble with escapes recently and they need some starch instilled in them. You leave tomorrow. That's all, Scully."

'This man was beginning to make cold rice pudding look good! If I had any sense I would have walked out of the door and kept on walking, but I knew that deserters fared worse than repeat criminals so I held my breath. Looking straight ahead, I stood as straight as I could and saluted him with an official "Yessir", before leaving his office. Outside I muttered to myself, "Bastard", before heading to my quarters to pack and prepare for the morrow.'

TWELVE

A change of direction

I MUST HAVE NODDED OFF LISTENING TO
Uncle John because when I opened my eyes the fire had burned
low and the gas lamps were hissing quietly in the background.
John sat opposite me staring into the fire, gazing at unseen
visions. For a man of his years, he still had all his faculties
about him.

'Sleep is the best medicine for someone who's drunk too
much grog', he said, still talking at glowing coals. 'And as
my old Uncle Mick used to say, "and it's horrid cheap, too."'
Smiling to himself, he turned to me. 'Sorry for boring you to
death, but when I get a captive audience I do tend to rattle
on – at least so my Maria says.'

'No, no, John', I protested loudly, sitting up straight in my
chair. 'Drink, good food, great company and an open hearth
are a sure fire way to send me into oblivion. If there was a
degree for sleeping Uncle John, then I reckon I'd be getting
high distinctions or honours!'

'Well, that sounds like something to sleep on', John replied.
'Happy Christmas, young man, and may the new year bring
you much happiness and a sense of where you are going, at

least.' With that, he heaved himself out of his chair, puffed up his cushion, tidied up around the room and left with our empty glasses. 'See you in the morning lad', and in a moment he was gone.

The new year came and with it the beginning of a new term. The law had desiccated my brain, even more so than the evenings in the pubs. A Dublin student's way of life had been a real eye-opener to a lad from the rural mid-west of the United States of America. Boy, did those Irish know how to have fun, and they knew how to have a good fight, too. I soon lost count of the number of nights which started out quietly with a few pints of beer and some great songs. Then, as things began to degenerate there would often be a bit of push and shove, before ending up outside on the pavement with a real wing-ding of fisticuffs. But you know what? Most times the lads went back inside, both sides bloodied and bruised, and called for one more for the road with the same fellows they'd only just been fighting with.

They were the sort of people that I found impossible not to love.

As winter moved into spring and my attendance at lectures was almost a sign for celebration amongst the teaching staff, I began to notice that although my grades were dropping off a cliff, the Irish lads I'd been carousing with were holding their own and still passing their exams. 'It's called balance, Frankie', one of my friends said, putting his arm around my shoulders as I read the list of exam results and failed to find my name in the pass section. 'The craic is great in Dublin but you don't want to go on believing that it'll get you a job or feed your family. Too many of the lads have families who've lived through the famine and that's an odious memory to have. You need to pace yourself lad. Celebrate your victories, drown your defeats but always turn up to the academic battle with the intention of winning every time. Otherwise you'll end up with the rest of the derelicts out there begging on the street. And believe me, it's bloody cold out there on a winter's night when everyone else has forgotten you.'

The guy stunned me. Was I really on the verge of being a Yankee alcoholic in Ireland? The thought smacked me between the eyes and stayed with me for hours as I wandered the streets, stopping now and then to stare into the dirty, dark Liffey flowing past me.

Over the next few weeks I did some serious soul-searching and came to the conclusion that a big part of the problem was that I really hated the law. Everything about it was as dry as a stick. But there was also a part of me that still couldn't see what was wrong with having a party every now and then. Believe me, there's nowhere like Dublin when you want to have a great party!

Amongst the students who knew how to let their hair down were the med students. In fact, they seemed to be the most extreme of the lot of them. There was the story of a severed arm being removed from the dissecting rooms, then concealed inside the sleeve of one student's coat. When it came time for this twisted romantic to leave his girlfriend on the park bench, he let it slide out behind them before making a swift exit. At the time I thought it was wickedly funny, but when the implications of it all sank in, I came to view it as idiotic and very wounding.

But overall the life of the medical student appealed, not only to my impish nature and my desire to enjoy what I was doing, but deep down, driving it all was an ambition to do something which would actually help people. In the end, the decision was made: the medical student life was going to be the life for me.

The Royal College of Surgeons stands proudly overlooking St Stephens Green at the top of Grafton Street. It's one of those grand old buildings built in the Greek style, with high Corinthian columns surmounted by a high fresco. It has a mighty history and has produced some world-famous physicians and surgeons. Interestingly, the building itself had been inspired by the French some centuries earlier. Now, it had become an esteemed part of the city and getting a place there was easier said than done. Naturally, entrance was by exam, yet it wasn't just what you knew but who you knew and how much money you had as well. I knew that I could manage two out of three but the entrance exam would mean a certain alteration to my indolent lifestyle.

I floated the idea with Uncle John, who was soon converted to my cause although Aunt Maria was less certain. 'Ah, Gosson', she said. 'Cutting up those corpses can't be good for your soul. What will the good Lord say to the poor creatures when they turn up at the pearly gates with half their parts scattered around the place?'

'The Civil War did more than scatter a few parts around the place, Aunt. It fair blasted the best men of my father's generation off the face of the planet', I replied soberly. Aunt Maria crossed herself saying, 'God bless the poor creatures', and she fell silent.

'I'll take you up there next week', John interrupted. 'I have a cousin who works there. You never know, it might prove handy if you want to take things further. But, my American bucko, you'll have to start giving some serious attention to the books if you're thinking about medicine. Mind you, there's some exciting stuff going on now with all this operating on people when they're put to sleep with ether. The Lord knows where it'll all lead to! You know, if I were a young man starting out in life, I'd give my right arm to be a doctor.'

'Did you hear that some mad eejit was given some other man's blood? They called it a trans*fus*ion', said Maria, prolonging the second syllable for effect. 'I call it total madness myself. She huffed herself into indignation. 'And there was some other mad old yoke who stuck a telescope into a part of a man's anatomy that shouldn't be discussed in polite company. The man must be possessed', she harrumphed.

'It's called an endoscope, I believe, my dear', John added soothingly. 'And I don't believe the man minded one jot once his bladder stone had been removed.'

'Bladder stone or no bladder stone, in my book there's no decent man should be doing that sort of thing to another man', and with that the conversation was over.

As the saying goes, we slept on it. Next day John and I hatched a little plot whereby he'd take me to meet his cousin at Surgeons and we'd see how things worked out from there. In the meantime, I said that I'd catch up with a few med students whom I'd met and have a chat with them.

The party scene continued but I must admit that I was a little more self-controlled. More and more I came to see that although the craic was mighty, as they say in Dublin, it came to have a certain sameness about it. Waking up with a hangover and the breath of a hog, with all your clothes stinking of tobacco and stale beer can hardly be described as the stuff of great deeds and a silken wit.

John and I visited Surgeons as arranged and we attended an operation, standing in the gallery with other interested parties including a few of my medical drinking companions. The sweetish smell of the open abdomen, the chemical smell of ether being dripped into the face mask over the unconscious patient, and the hiss of the gas lights all added to the great theatre of the event.

'I heard tell of a Yankee surgeon in the Civil War who could cut off a leg in under three minutes.'

'What happened to the patient?' John whispered back to me.

'I suppose he died', I surmised. 'I don't suppose that bothered the surgeon though. Most of their patients seem to die anyway.'

'Well I heard of a Dr Liston in London who could take a man's leg off in two and a half minutes. And there was an unfortunate man who had his testicles removed along with his leg in another of those speedy operations.' John nudged me to re-gain my attention. 'They both died, too. But I hear that Dr Lister has discovered that using carbolic acid sprays reduces the morbid sepsis that happens after nearly all surgical procedures.'

'Did someone just mention carbolic acid and that fool Lister?' The surgeon spoke out, having removed his knife from between his teeth where he was holding it as he reached for a clamp. 'The man's a heretic. Knows nothing of medicine. Should be kicked out of the profession.' He stood there in his frock coat, sleeves rolled up, and dared anyone to challenge him.

Afterwards, as we walked down the steps and across the road into Stephens Green I asked John whether he agreed with the surgeon about Dr Lister.

'I'm not sure Frankie', he mused. 'But from what I read he does seem to have produced some impressive results with his new sprays. Post-surgery mortality down from forty-five percent to fifteen percent. You can't argue with that. Mind you, he did say that ether anaesthetic would be as safe as houses too, but that's not always the case.' We sat down on a park bench to enjoy the rare Dublin sunshine. 'But I must say that it's an exciting time to be in medicine. If you think that Her Majesty the Queen had chloroform to help her having her babies and now it's all the rage in London. That sort of thing would have been unthinkable just twenty years ago.' We both lapsed into silence and watched the pigeons, pretending to pick at worms as they slyly approached our feet hoping that perhaps we might have some bread in our pockets.

It was decided that if I could improve my scores in the last term of law then we would see if I could secure a place at Surgeons.

'What shall I tell the old man back home?' I asked John.

The good man smiled. 'It's often a better idea to seek for-giveness than to seek permission. So my suggestion would be to get yourself a place at Surgeons and then tell him of your great news. Tell him that you've talked it through with me and I thought it a good idea, too. I'm not sure whether that will be a help or a hindrance but at least it'll make him pause and consider before doing anything rash like cutting off your allowance.'

It had never occurred to me that father would do such a thing. In a flash, I realised how fragile my position really was.

'Looks like I'd better do some study then', I added ruefully.

'Wouldn't do you any harm', was John's quick riposte.

I returned to the law faculty and buckled down to the mind-numbing routine of studying law, governance, property rights and criminal law. The last subject was the one that aroused a lot a passion in class, especially as some of the Irish students from outside the Pale had long and obvious grievances about how British law was administered in their country.

One summer evening, after such a class when some of the establishment students and the Fenian students had nearly come to blows, I asked John if he'd heard of a Mr Parnell. 'He's part Yankee and I heard tell he visited our southern states recently', I said. 'I also hear he's a great talker and is putting the cat amongst the pigeons with all his talk of Home Rule for Ireland. Do you think it will ever happen in your lifetime?'

'I can't see it happening for some time yet, Frankie. Her Majesty's Government is sucking on a lot of teats around the world and losing any one of them could have a devastating domino effect for her empire. Here, India, Africa …' He fell silent searching for the right words.

'The auld British Empire has done great things over the years, but it's also been a massive curse on the poor people who've been subjugated to its will.' It was one of those gorgeous Irish summer evenings where the sun lingers in the air like the music from a favourite ballad.

'In New South Wales, we inherited the very best and the very worst of colonial rule. The trouble was that the rules were just as strict on the enforcers as they were on their charges.'

THIRTEEN

Hassan's Wall

'I'D BARELY HAD TIME TO BECOME AC-quainted with any of the citizens of Windsor. In some respects it reminded me a little of the better villages in County Limerick, except that at that particular time of year there was a distinct lack of green about the place. But Easter was coming and the worst of the blast of heat was over. With the promise of rain I could see that the older settlers scanned the skies for rain clouds and they laughed more easily.

'I was to relieve a Lieutenant McDonald of the 28th who was under the command of Captain Moore at Coxs River. My detachment consisted of an assistant surgeon and two privates, modest by anyone's standards, but for me it was as grand an army as Wellington's at Waterloo.

'We travelled on foot as there was no horse for a mere lieutenant and definitely none for the privates, so it took a couple of days slow marching before we crossed the Blue Mountains in order to reach the stockade. But the hardships of walking were more than compensated for by the views along the way. They were breathtaking, and believe you me, when it's hot in the Blue Mountains, then the mountains really are blue. They say it's due to the oil from the eucalyptus trees hanging in the air. Whatever, it's a sight you never forget.

'We arrived at the end of March and walked up to the stockade. Even though it had only been there for a couple of years, it had the air of a military barracks, yet it also had a homely feel to it. I suppose that was because of the surrounding forests, and sound of the Coxs River running close by. Later on I was to learn that in the cold of winter, all sense of hominess was driven out by the damp and bitter nights. In fact, I seem to recall that during winter, my assistant surgeon was busier than the guards dealing with chest infections and consumptive coughs.

'I met with Lieutenant Mc Donald and he briefly gave me details of the stockade. There were 143 convicts in the iron gangs along with twelve servants and artificers out of irons. The convicts were held in "boxes", as they called them. Primitive caravans like the tinkers use back home. Except of course these were a lot bigger. Each box could accommodate between eighteen and twenty-four convicts. I suppose they must have been about fourteen feet long and roughly eight foot wide.

'The convicts slept on the floor or on one of the two shelves inside. Hardly the stuff of luxury. The later versions came with wheels on, so as the road continued to move west, the boxes could follow them. It was supposed to save time and money of course, but I doubt it made much difference really. It would have been better if we had more horses and carts, but then the honchos back in London were savage on a pound and were taking money away from us instead of giving us the resources we really needed.

'When I came to know some of the stories about these people it made me wonder why on earth some of them had been sent to the other side of the world for stealing a shawl in the middle of winter in rural Ireland. Or why a young lad from London had been sent there for stealing cheese, or a maid for stealing herrings, or another lad for taking one single piece of fruit or pork or bacon, whatever. I'm telling you Frankie, there was no sense to it at all.

'It was hard work out there on the western highway. Digging, crushing, hammering every day in all sorts of weather. You can understand why some of them thought they'd be better off with the natives. But it wasn't just the poor ironed gangs that suffered. My men were at their wits' end.

'You've got to remember, most of the ordinary soldiers were little better than the convicts they were guarding. In fact, they had a great deal in common. They were often dirt poor and uneducated, and the only reason they weren't in prison was because they were in the army. The poor creatures had to rouse and then guard the convicts all day, and then stand guard over them all night.

'I might have been stationed at Hassan's Wall, but I also had charge of Bowens Hollow Stockade a few miles away where they quarried stone for the bridge nearby. Thank God the bridge was finished and Bowens was being run down, but there were still convicts there under the command of a sergeant and an overseer. Mind you, I didn't even have a horse to travel between the two spots! Looking back, I suppose I put too much trust in the sergeant, but what else could I do?

'On top of all that, being an officer meant that I had to regularly present myself for jury duty at the Supreme Court in Sydney. The upshot of that was that I had to absent myself from Hassan's and head up to Sydney, leaving a junior in charge. Talk about the blind leading the blind!

'Then a couple of men absconded. Thomas Muskelly and John Cumming were the men's' names and I can see their faces as if they were standing here in front of me.

'The two of them were in an ironed gang, at Hassan's Wall, and were wheeling their carts loaded with rocks on the public road when they decided to rush upon poor little William Quick – now there's an oxymoron of a name for you – and disarm him of his musket. The mounted police found them in double quick time – if you'll excuse my pun. In their defence they said that they'd been driven to the act in consequence of the severe treatment they had met with from those employed over them in the gang. Which, as I can tell you was a load of old bollocks, as they say here in Dublin.

'The verdict was a foregone conclusion: the jury found the prisoners guilty, and the court ordered judgment of death to be recorded against them. It was all very sad, very sad indeed. It was made worse by the fact that I had to reprimand poor old Quick who was just doing his job! Then, to add insult to injury, I had to face the wrath of that bastard Nunn back in Windsor, not that he was doing his reputation much good about that time.

'The unholy Nunn was now spending as much time in Sydney as he was in Windsor. He was a career man and no doubt wanted to get as close to Colonel Snodgrass as he could. There's an Irish expression for men such as he, but I don't think it should be used in polite company. But his story of outrageous treachery needs to be told.

'In September and November 1837, four white servants were murdered by natives. Knowing what I do now, I suspect that it was in retaliation for having their lands and their women stolen from them. But the local settlers in the area decided

to write a petition to the government requesting better protection. Enter our infamous Major James Nunn. He was despatched to the area with twenty-three mounted police. Yes,
that's right, twenty-three men with guns, on horses, against
men on foot with spears and clubs. His orders were for each
man to "react according to his own judgment, and use his
utmost exertion to suppress these outrages".

'Dunn found and arrested fifteen Aborigines and released
all but two, one of whom was shot whilst attempting to escape.
It's hard to imagine an armed man on a horse needing to
shoot dead a man who was only armed with a spear at best.
Be that as it may, the main body of natives eluded the troopers, so our brave Major Nunn's party along with two stockmen pursued them for three weeks until they found them on
the upper Gwydir River.

'On the morning of January 26, in a surprise attack on
Nunn's party, Corporal Hannan was wounded in the leg with a
spear and in retaliation four or five Aborigines were shot dead.
The rest of them fled down the river as the troopers regrouped,
rearmed, and pursued them, led by the second-in-command,
Lieutenant George Cobban. Our George was a fine piece of
work, too. Straight out of Major Nunn's handbook on how
to be a model officer!

'Cobban's party found their quarry about a mile down the
river, where a second engagement took place. The encounter
lasted several hours, and no Aborigines were captured. Can
you believe that? Not one native survived!

'According to Georgie Cobban, in his official report he said,
"Perhaps two were shot in the initial engagement and three
or four bodies were in the bush." That didn't tally with what
Sergeant John Lee reported. He was with the main group

and claimed that forty to fifty of them were badly killed. But who do you believe? A missionary, Lancelot Threkeld, thought the number to be about 120. There was even a report several days later that the bodies of over 300 men, women and children were found in a nearby swamp – a number unmatched in other recorded massacres in Australia. They were reputedly killed over a period of three days.

'So after this glorious victory what did the powers that be do? They renamed the creek "Waterloo", recalling Britain's victory of 1815 over Napoleon. Major Nunn was heard later on to boast of "popping off with his holster pistols at the blacks whenever one appeared from behind a tree". That was not a very diplomatic thing to do in the polite circles of Sydney and it soon got to the ears of the new Governor, Sir George Cripps, who was horrified. According to him and the British Government, "Aborigines are British Subjects, not to be killed with impunity by Her Majesty's forces of law and order."

'Sadly, that didn't change much on the ground. No investigation into the massacre was held until April 1839, and guess what? The good major and his men were never legally tried. But by God, I remember what happened; and I will never forget what happened to those poor men women and children.

FOURTEEN

Do unto others

EVERY SUNDAY WE ATTENDED THE LOCAL parish church for Mass. For a reprobate Yankee like myself, I felt a power of guilt kneeling down amongst these good folk. Everyone was dressed in their Sunday best and there were children everywhere and all silent as lambs. But like life itself, under those clothes, behind the masks on those faces were complex human beings with their fears, their hopes; their desires for themselves and their desires for revenge; their pig-headedness, their stupidity and their goodness. I am certain that there were a few saints amongst them too.

Everyone seemed to be wearing black except the priest who wore bright green regalia and said the rubrics in Latin with his back turned to us. Bells rang, incense billowed into the musty, barren chapel and the only sounds to be heard were the muffled words and the shuffling of feet. It seemed as if the whole process was to denude the imagination of any idea of paradise by the sheer bleakness of it all. Then the priest would turn to give his sermon.

On my first visit to this particular church, I sat in gloomy anticipation on the ice-cold pew thinking that perhaps hell might offer an intriguing alternative, and looked around me to see if anyone else might be thinking the same. There was not a single sign of redemption to be seen.

'Most of us here would understand the expression, "When hell freezes over".'

The man was looking straight at me. He then proceeded to dissect the Gospel readings with great insight and even managed to raise some life out of his half-conscious congregation. Within ten minutes he'd finished. I was gob-smacked, to use a local expression.. I leaned very slightly in John's direction and whispered as quietly as I could. 'The man's a genius. How did he know I was thinking those things?'

'Shhh', Maria hissed from my other side, nudging me in the ribs.

When we left the church, pausing to dip our fingers into the chilly fonts to bless ourselves, Father was at the main door to greet us. 'Ah, so this is your American nephew come to visit us, John? And how are ye surviving the onslaught of another man in the house, Maria? Eating you out of house and home yet?'

'So far so good, Father, though he has his head stuck in the law and it's giving the lad the dickens of a headache', John proffered.

'It hasn't affected his appetite though, Father', trilled Maria.

'Ah, the law! This country has had a good dose of the law for too long, don't you think John? Time we tried something else eh? There's a real hunger around and I'm not just talking about their stomachs! Listen to your heart lad. If you're anything like your uncle and aunt here, it must be almost pure gold.'

'You're damn right there, Father', I blurted. Before I had the chance to blush, the man burst out laughing, causing those nearby to turn their heads and stare at us.

John and Maria teased me on our short walk home and by the time the dolphin had knocked itself back into place on the front door, I was sitting in the kitchen staring out at the view of the park.

'Here Frankie, read this', John said, having rummaged through some draws before finding what he was looking for. 'It's the legal system at work in Australia. Ring any bells?'

I took the fragile, yellowing sheets of newspaper in my hands. It was a copy of *The Australian*, dated 14 August 1838. On page two I read the opening paragraphs, which were obviously written by a most exuberant reporter.

DOMESTIC INTELLIGENCE – SOLDIERS AND CONVICTS

The disclosures that took place on the trial of the four soldiers of the 80th regiment for highway robbery, are certainly of the most alarming nature, and demand – what we have no doubt they will receive – the most earnest attention of the government. The officers of the stockades in that vicinity ought to undergo the most rigid examination as to the discipline that has been kept up …

I turned to page three where the story unfolded further.

… Not only among the convicts but among the soldiers. At Bowens Hollow Stockade it appears it was not considered necessary to place a commissioned officer as Hassan's Wall, where there were either two or three officers, was only three miles off. The fact of the soldiers at an ironed gang conspiring with the convicts under charge, unlocking the prison door, taking the men out, assisting them to take off their irons, and committing robberies by means of the firearms that were placed in their hands for the protection of the public, is most alarming. That we may not be accused of exaggeration we will lay before our readers the evidence.

There followed a detailed report of the questioning of the various witnesses and the cross-examination of the defendants, revealing evidence so damning that there could only be one verdict.

His Honour summed up at a late hour, and the jury having retired for about ten minutes returned a verdict of guilty against the prisoners. His Honour desired proclamation to be made and briefly addressed the prisoners on the aggravated enormity of the offence of which they had been found guilty situated as they were as guards over the convicts and wearing the uniform of Her Majesty. It was their duty to set an example to the unhappy men over whom they were placed, instead of which they had joined them in their lawless pursuits; had furnished them with fire arms which had been entrusted to them for the preservation of the public peace, to rob the traveller. He would not hold out any hopes of mercy being extended to them, as it was necessary that an awful example should be made, to prevent, if possible, similar breaches of the important trust placed in the soldiers. He would not say that the doors of mercy were closed against them – but that rested with a higher power, and he would not have them indulge any hope of it. His Honour then passed the sentence of death on the prisoners, to be carried into effect at His Excellency's pleasure.

I finished reading the paper and rested it on my knee. There was a deep silence in the room and the atmosphere had become one shade darker.

'Those were my men', John said. 'I can't defend them: they were rogues, there's no doubt about that. They lied, they cheated, and they were lazy, too, but Pike could tell a yarn that would make a nun wet herself with laughter.' He smiled. 'I can assure you, that watching a young man hang is a terrible thing.' The weak sunlight disappeared behind a blackened cloud, and the sound of a stretching sisal rope seemed to haunt that darkened room.

FIFTEEN

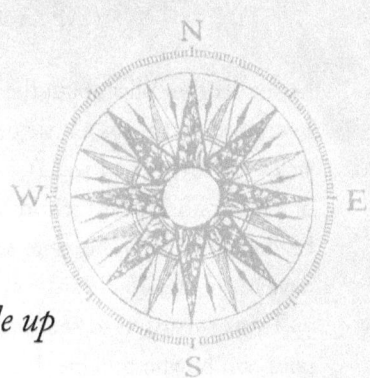

My mind is made up

I LOOKED OVER AT JOHN. MARIA BUSTLED back into the room and reached for her apron. 'Get out of here lads, there's real work to be done preparing a decent meal for ye', and we were shooed from the kitchen into the corridor.

Taking our seats by the kindling new fire which had been left laid in the grate, John continued his story.

'The work at Hassan's Wall was slowing and the roadworks were steadily moving to other areas. I was being forced to work with fewer men and more responsibility in a remote location far away from any support or advice. I was twenty-seven years of age.

'I'd spent months afloat having to cope with my own countrymen being locked up like savages. I'd had to order floggings, I'd witnessed hangings which still shattered my sleep, and I was under the command of some people who I wouldn't trust with spent cartridge. I was literally at my wits' end.

'About that time, I'd been recalled to Windsor on some forgettable but highly military mission – probably to say that we should shorten the length of the men's leg chains as the price of iron had gone up and the bigwigs in London were getting hot under the collar about the cost of it all. Thinking on it now I suppose that I was a little depressed, perhaps a little home-sick too, leastways, I wasn't sure which way to turn. I'd heard of a new parish priest who'd recently arrived in the town, so I headed down to his house to seek his guidance and maybe even have my confession heard. I can't remember the details exactly.

'I was surprised to see that his cottage was occupied by a poor family, who told me that the good man himself was living in the lean-to shed at the side of the house. 'Come in', the big lump of a man said when I knocked on the shed door. My first impression was that he was a few years older than me, though his eyes sparkled with youthful delight at the sight of company.

'"How are ye, Father?" I said, removing my hat and placing it under my left arm. "Did I detect a Cavan accent there?"

'"Perhaps, Captain", he replied, reaching out a ham of a hand to grasp mine. "John Brady from Carrickatober, although the accent isn't pure Cavan. Come in, come in", he urged, and I followed him into the gloom. Though it was hot and sunny outside, inside of Father Brady's shed it was even hotter. I was instantly reminded of those convict cabins that I knew so well and wondered why a man of the cloth should choose to live under such circumstances. Certainly his accommoda-tion was a far cry from most of the other clergy I had known in my lifetime.

'Shafts of white light speared the gloom through the shrunken, wooden, wall slats. When Father Brady seated himself on his small stool, his blond hair fairly shone in its rays. "Welcome to my humble abode", he began. "I'm sorry but I didn't get your name."

'"Captain John Scully", I replied formally. "But the accent's pure Tip, Father." I looked for somewhere to place my hat. Finding none, I put it on the earth floor next to me.

'Reading my mind as my eyes adjusted to the gloom, John Brady jerked his thumb in the direction of his former cottage next door. "They need it more than me, Captain. They have a small family and they keep the place clean and tidy. It suits us both." He looked down at his hands. "There should be enough to go round for all, but human nature …" His voice drifted off. "And how may I help you, Captain?"

"'John", I interjected. "Please call me John, Father. Every man and his dog calls me Captain and yet it's like the rest of the uniform – it's all a performance really." My eyes landed on his long black soutane and I quickly added, "Present company excepted, eh, Father?"

'Father Brady wasn't a stupid man. In fact, he was quite a brilliant man in many ways. He spoke three languages fluently as far as I knew – French, Gaelic and Latin – as well as English, and he had a good smattering of Greek as well. I also suspect, though I never really discovered if it was true, that there was something in the good man's accent that reminded me of a Russian I'd met at John's drinking den in Sydney. He was a strange paradox of earnestness, innocence and other-worldliness. But I liked the man and he put me at my ease. I told him the reason that I was there and he listened in his simple way and nodded calmingly when I began to get agitated.

"'We see some cruel things, don't we, we so-called civilised Christians. We do things in the name of law and order which seem neither legal nor orderly. I wonder what our master would say if he appeared in Parliament in London, or indeed at St Peter's in Rome." He gave a snorting chuckle and fell silent, indicating that I should continue.

'I finished my list of concerns and as an afterthought asked if he would hear my confession, too.

"I doubt you can have much more to confess, John", he smiled back at me as he reached for his accoutrements. He settled himself as the light-illuminated motes danced around his blond hair making him appear almost beautiful. I was struck by a sense that he was a holy man and this would be a holy moment. He laid his hands on my head in absolution of my simple sins, and the sense of relief inside me as his hands lifted from my head was sublime. That moment is as real to me now as it was all those years ago. I cherish that confession and the memory of a good and simple priest. The poor man was to suffer greatly afterwards and was nearly driven mad by certain people in the Swan River Settlement. But that was many years later. For now, he worked as a simple priest – doing his best to save souls where he saw the need.

"Are you here for long John?" he asked as he folded his stole and put it away safely.

"No, Father. Just for a couple of days. I have to see the major tomorrow to hand in my resignation. Will you be around for long?"

'John Brady snorted his chuckle saying, "I only wish. I set off tomorrow to see a family who's doing it tough up near Penrith. It's a mighty big stretch of land I have to look after and there's many a man and good woman who need some spiritual support in these hard times." He sat there as if seeing the families he would be visiting shortly and it took me aback a little when he said, "Have you heard of the settlement out in the west, John? It's called the Swan River Settlement. I'm hearing some interesting things about it. It's pretty remote but they say there's great potential out there. If I was a fine strapping young fellow like you with a bit of money to spare, I could be quite tempted to take my chances." His eyes held mine for a moment. "And they don't have convicts over there, either."

'He stood up and tried to stretch, but his lumpy frame was cramped in by the leaning roof of the shed. "Well, I must prepare for my trip tomorrow. The devil and idle hands, eh, John." Reaching out his hand he took mine in his and with deep affection said, "Good you meet you. You never know, we might even meet up over in Western Australia, wouldn't that be a laugh, eh?"

'"Hilarious"', I replied happily. "You could be the bishop and I could be the Colonial Secretary." At which he snorted a loud, long laugh. Little did either of us know how close to the truth that jest really was.'

SIXTEEN

On the seas again

'THE 80TH HAD ITS HEADQUARTERS UP AT Windsor, yet most of our troops were dispersed throughout New South Wales. Communication back then was not always easy or reliable. One person who never failed though was my mother, who was the most loyal of correspondents. Every month when the mail arrived I was certain to receive a letter from Tipperary in her familiar handwriting. Her letters were full of family news and gossip from our staff. She never alluded to it directly, yet reading between the lines, I could discern that she was worried about my father's health. Being the third son has both advantages and disadvantages. One of the advantages is that the trials and tribulations of being a parent had been finely honed on my two elder brothers, leaving me perhaps an easier path in my childhood.

'Father was a good man and much loved in the community. But he was a strict disciplinarian, which had its advantages and disadvantages!

'He had to be strict with us because as well as being a banker, for forty years he'd been the senior magistrate in the whole of Tipperary. If any of his boys had stepped out of line in any way he would have been mortified. That's why the first of us were tutored at home and the younger ones sent off to Downside to board away from the eyes of the locals. Just in case!

'Father was a fair man, a diligent and decent man. Although he worked long hours, he still found time to enjoy himself. I loved the dear man and had great respect for him. Looking back over the years I suppose he was the ideal role model for a lad who could easily have idled his life away. It was because of him that I was to take up the life of Resident Magistrate in Australia and continued in that career when I returned to Galway.

'Mother had indicated in a letter shortly after the regiment had arrived in New South Wales that there were changes afoot in the family's Joint Stock Bank – the bank that my father had inherited from Grandfather. My eldest brother James was expected to take over when he turned thirty, but James's heart wasn't really in the banking business. He was a lot like my father. He was much more interested in the land and serving as a magistrate.

'Anyway, a nephew of ours by marriage, name of Sadlier, had been talking to James and there was talk of expanding the bank. I didn't know too much about what was going on and knew even less about John Sadlier apart from the fact that he was family. In her letters, Mother had told me that John was a successful lawyer in Dublin, and it was he who was pushing the idea of expanding the bank. At the time he was aged about twenty-seven. If I'd known then what I know now, then … well, there's no point trying to change the past.

'Mother sent me a letter telling me that Father wasn't in the best of form. It wasn't what she wrote, but what she hadn't written that concerned me the most. I was also under pressure from James who wanted me to come home and talk about the bank. It all happened around the time of the Hassan's Wall trial and what with the way the major had been treating me, I decided that the time was right for me to hand in my resignation and head home to see what I could do there. Besides, I missed the green of this beautiful country. The thought of another summer of blistering heat and humidity in New South Wales certainly didn't hold too much attraction for me at that stage.

'I read my mother's letter several times and decided to literally sleep on it before I made any decision.

'Next morning, 19 June 1838, with my mind fully made up, I went to Major Nunn and handed in my resignation.

'From the distracted expression on his face it seemed he'd been expecting it anyhow.

'"Thank you Captain", was all he said. "You may as well take it to Sydney with you when you leave. It'll probably get there quicker that way", he said. The man never even lifted his head from what he was doing before handing my letter back to me.

'I was in two minds as to whether to call him the bastard he was or just turn and leave, but he beat me to it. He paused writing, pen suspended mid-sentence, lifted his eyes towards me – and I can still see the arrogant expression on his face – and asked as meek as you like: "Is there anything else, Captain Scully?"

'For a few seconds we held each other's gaze, daring one another to say something.

'I'm embarrassed to report that I was the one to back down. That's another of the downsides of being the third son: from the moment you become aware of your surroundings, you always find yourself giving in to people – especially bullies.

My life in the military had also taught me one fundamental fact about surviving in the army: hold your tongue to people in power over you.

'I saluted the man silently, turned on my heel and left, dropping the wooden latch as loudly as I could in a pathetic sign of revenge. Talking of heels, I had to cool mine for a few days longer. I was a civilian now and had no horse of my own and it was pointless to buy one just to travel to Sydney. So I waited for transport to take me south. I had to wait a few days because the recent storms had washed the road out in several places making it impassable for any transport.

'I planned to stay in Sydney until I could find a berth to Ireland so I decided to look up David and see if he could recommend somewhere for me to stay.

'"Dear boy, I wouldn't dream of it", he exclaimed, his eyebrows shooting up on his face, and the fat of his chin wobbling merrily below it." No, no, no, NO dear boy, you will stay with me and we'll have nice chats when I get home from work." David brooked no dissent, and in a strange sort of way I was happy to be taken in by him. Sure, he was a strange character and he didn't conceal the furtive smiles he sent certain young men who, in return, flashed back their understanding of him with a twitch of their own eyes. But with me he was just a good, kind, and generous man who only wanted to help out where he could, so I agreed and arranged to meet him at his house later that day.

'I told him that I had to go to headquarters to deliver my resignation but would be back shortly. "I'm so glad you're getting out, John", he soothingly said, patting me on the arm. "Those soldiers are so rough and some of their officers ..." He let the sentence hang in the air as his eyes rolled up in mock horror. "Very unsavoury creatures some of them are, and believe me I've met a lot of unpleasant people in my time." I left dear David and went about my business before returning to his house.

'It was deserted when I returned. Stuck to the front door was a message with my name upon it.

Dear Friend,

Good news. You might be interested to learn of a cabin on the Ganges which is to depart at the end of this month. Suggest you go down to the docks and discuss details with its master one Malcolm MacDonald. He's a good man, though don't let him near the rum too often as he's a man after my own HEART.

Call down to the tavern once you've settled yourself in. Key in the usual spot!

David

P.S. I hope you like the smell of whale oil!

'Needless to say, John has a mighty sense of humour.

'I let myself in and washed the dust from my face before heading down to the harbour to find Captain MacDonald. It's almost fifty years ago now and nothing happened quickly back then. Anything to do with ships, the sea and travelling half way around the world, well, you wouldn't want to be in a hurry! The captain was a kindly man who reported that he'd given away the grog. "It was eating the guts out of me" were his exact words and you have to admire anyone who gives it away just like that.

'Malcolm was a shy, insular sort of figure really, and like all sailors, had leathered, beaten skin with rheumy eyes which belied his years. He sported the regulation white, well-trimmed beard. In what looked to be a yellowed nest surrounding a mouth with yellowed teeth sprouted a clay pipe devoid of any smoke.

'Removing his pipe and spitting overboard, he told me, "I have a cabin for you, Captain. David said you might be down." He eyed me to see if I might belong to the unnerving company of men that John was known to associate with. I gripped his hand hard in acknowledgement and returned his gaze. As if acknowledging my unspoken response he gave a slight nod of his head which told me that he understood. "Not sure when we'll get away", he continued, searching each pocket of his faded uniform jacket in search of his pouch of tobacco. "Depends when we fill the holds with produce. Shouldn't be too long though." Having filled his pipe, his eyes moved to the barrels of whale oil being rolled down the plank and onto the deck. "Mind 'ow you go there lads!" he shouted. "That there's your wages when you get to the old country!"

'Captain McDonald was right to be unsure as to when we'd set sail. In fact, we didn't get underway until 8 July when the winds were right and the holds full of wool and sperm oil. Thank God my cabin was to the rear of the boat because the smell of that cargo was as thick as tar and twice as nauseous when I first went on board. Strange to say, though, that within three days of sailing, the smell never crossed my mind again. We're odd creatures, aren't we?

'What can I say about the trip? The trip down the east coast was fast as we had good winds but when we hit the straits between the mainland and Van Diemen's Land we were fairly belted by heavy seas and mighty winds. I think everyone on board became well-acquainted with the insides of their stomach on that section. But Hobart was a nice place. It has a busy port and the English settlers have done a fine job reproducing their homeland. We took a day trip out to Richmond which is about ten miles from the main settlement and I found it a lot like the old country.

'There were no natives on that island and oddly, most people seemed reluctant to talk about what had happened to them. After discreet inquiry I was to learn of their tragic story. In short, early on in the piece, Governor Davy had seen fit to rid the island of its "savages". After a number of horrific slaughters, he'd packed the remnants off to another small island where I hear they are now slowly perishing from neglect and broken hearts.

'Just imagine how you'd feel if all we Irish were packed off and sent to live on the Island of Iona.

'That's Van Diemen's Land for you. Beautiful, full of promise but with a haunting legacy of sadness. I suppose they'll get over it one day, but by God I reckon that's still a long, long time away.

'From Hobart we went direct to the Cape and on to home. Sea travel has its own rhythm, but it teaches you patience and it reminds you how small we really are: vulnerable too. One sailor died along the way. No-one really knew why. He was such a healthy lad and he shouldn't have died …

'Once we got back to the low, grey skies of an Irish springtime I headed straight back to the auld country and down to Tipperary. The smell of turf being burned on the fire, the sight of green fields, green trees and fat, white, fluffy sheep in those fields made me almost weep with happiness. I was so excited as we walked down those familiar streets and up to our old, familiar front door. For an instant it was almost as if I'd never left. But something had changed.

'Me.'

SEVENTEEN

Blood, sweat and fears!

A TELEGRAM ARRIVED AT ANGLESEA Road addressed to me. It was from my pa in the US. He'd obviously received my letter telling him of my plans to study medicine. The telegram was fairly succinct: 'You stop studying law, I stop paying your allowance'. With those ten words it became crystal clear that the ice I was skating on here in Dublin had suddenly become dangerously thin! 'John', I called down the garden to where the good man had secured himself in the safety of his small shed. It was what he described as a 'dacent' distance from the all-seeing eyes of Maria.

'I think you should read this.' I pushed the door of the shed open and walked into a fug of aromatic pipe smoke. John was seated on a tall stool reading through some yellowed papers that he'd rescued from a battered old sea chest. I handed him the telegram and waited.

He perched there on his stool and a smile crept over his face and his twinkling eyes lifted to meet my own. He handed me the thin paper back and said, 'Exactly what I'd have done myself.' He clutched his pipe in his hand and clasped his elbow with the other. 'Just wait though', he went on. 'He just needs time.'

He dropped what he was reading and out of the blue asked, 'You never talk about your dear mother. Whatever happened to the poor woman?'

What indeed had happened to her? I scavenged around in my brain seeking out snippets of stories that I'd hidden in the crevices of my mind. I stared at the yellowed paper in John's hand. 'I suppose she was too good for this world. Sounds trite doesn't it? It's the sort of thing pastors say at funerals. In fact, it's what the pastor did say at her funeral. But you know what? It's true. Mom had a sort of translucence to her. She spoiled me. You know, I remember once when I'd gotten into trouble with Pa and he'd sent me to my room, Mom crept around to my window and tapped ever so lightly on it to check that I was OK. She had a gentle soul. The docs out home called it hysteria. Said it was because she was a woman and they suffered in the mind because of that. But deep inside of her there was a black void which no light could illuminate. We all tried – even Pa tried – but when she was sad, no-one could reach her.'

The quiver of the papers John was holding had almost ceased. 'What happened son?' he asked oh-so-gently.

'She went missing one day. A kindly neighbour found her wandering near their ranch a mile or two away from home. He's a good Christian man and he stopped to she if she was fine, which she wasn't, so he drove her back to our homestead in his buggy. Promised not to say a word and he hasn't ever broken that promise as far as I know. To his credit, Pa was as gentle with her as if she were the frailest lamb ever born anywhere in this world. But she just sat there and stared out the window and didn't speak to no one. Pa wrote to her folks in New York, and in the end he decided to take her back there for some sort of treatment, leaving us in the care of my eldest brother. It transpired that her folk had contacts with the best and brightest doctors in the land.'

I heaved a deep sigh. 'But by all accounts it didn't make a jot of difference. Ma faded away and died. Melancholy. That's what it said on the certificate. Broken heart more likely', I said, feeling the blood rise in my gorge. 'We all let her down. Pa should have known better.'

'Whoa there lad', John soothed. 'Life's not always that simple.' Rain began to tap on the tin roof of the shed. 'Life has a beginning, a middle and an end. And death either comes too soon or too late, but it never arrives on time! Your ma died too young, I agree with that. And you suffered really badly, and it's not right that any child should have to go through such things – but it happens. But pointing the finger of blame never brings relief.' He paused. 'Have you ever asked your ma to forgive you? Have you ever thought that she might like to ask for your forgiveness? Come to think of it, have you ever thought of asking your pa those same questions?'

The rain stopped as swiftly as it had begun. The sun came out and a shaft of light smiled through the smeared widow.

'By the way, whatever happened to that lass you met on the boat? The one you were so coy about when you first arrived?'

The man was a genius!

Blushing to the roots of my hair, I shrugged my shoulders and pushed my hands deep into my pockets as if trying to push my feelings into them, too. 'Not much', I mumbled. 'Haven't really had time to go and look for her.'

A rumbling chuckle began in his lower regions, rose up through his chest and silently rocked his shoulders. 'Say no more', was all the good man said. 'Say no more.'

The truth was that I'd never stopped thinking about Mary Nash. She'd grown in my mind and my imagination even though I'd not set eyes on her since arriving in Dublin. Naturally, I'd chased other girls as every self-righteous Dublin lad does after swallowing a few pints of mother's milk – as the locals call Arthur Guinness's well-known tipple. And I'd been rejected by nearly all of them, too. 'I've be courted by a better class of lecher than you, my lad', was one reply that stuck in my conscience: but the gist of the message was always the same from most of those good, and not-so-good lasses.

The mention of Mary Nash confused my mind. I mumbled some apology and left John to his tin shed and his trips down memory lane. I went up to my room – accompanied by two thick ham sandwiches which Maria had given me as I walked through the kitchen. 'Just to keep body and soul together, son', she had winked. There in my splendid isolation I took a big bite from my sandwich and began to think.

John and Maria had been better than family to me since my arrival. They'd tolerated my late nights and later mornings. Maria never uttered a single complaint as she gathered my booze-soaked clothes and washed them in the copper out in the little laundry lean-to. John never judged me when, as so often happened, the monthly tab at the local pub exceeded the allowance sent to me from Pa in America. Perhaps it was because they'd never had a chance to have children, or maybe it was because they were just good and decent folk. I even began to realise that although Pa had been tough on me, he was under no legal obligation to pay for my education in Ireland. Many were the lads who worked night jobs as hospital orderlies just to make ends meet and yet here was me living the good life and taking no responsibility for it.

And then there was Mary Nash.

Our first meeting had not gone well. I was an arrogant but frightened young man trying to prove to the world what a suave guy I was. She was vulnerable and alone and very drunk on the two glasses of sherry I'd shared with her. Even now the memory of the smell of her vomit caused me to sniff at my sleeve. Deep down, there was something inside me that whispered that I'd met the woman of my life. But how could I possibly think of stepping out with her when all I'd achieved was to be a failed law student and a successful drunk!

Luckily for me, Pa's telegram had arrived early on in the month so I had a few weeks' breathing space to start getting my act together. The first step in that direction was to go and find Mary Nash and see if she'd even remember me.

'Right!' I said aloud to myself. 'Time for a bit of good old Yankee spit and polish and I'll be irresistible!' Even as I said the words, my heart leapt into my mouth and began pulsing a drum beat of doubt. I looked in the small mirror and asked, 'She will remember me … won't she?'

I dressed as smartly as I could, splashed some cologne around my neck, gave my hair one parting caress and went downstairs.

Maria's eyes shot up like two unrestrained blinds. 'Off out, is it?' she asked, pummelling a pile of dough into shape before beating it flat again.

'There's lecture on at 5 which I don't want to miss', I lied blatantly.

'Ah yes', came my aunt's reply. She picked up the dough and raised it above her head before dramatically dropping it like the blade of a guillotine, saying, 'A lecture!' The sound of the dough hitting the floured board remained with me after I'd closed the door behind me. But the sense of guilt at having lied to her stayed with me until I stood outside the imperial entrance to the Coombe Lying-in Hospital where Mary worked. Just the look of the place scared the wits out of me.

I adjusted my tie and behind my back clasped a bunch of violets that I'd bought from a frowsy vendor in Grafton Street. I asked the porter whether he knew of a Mary Nash.

'Mary Nash', he returned, studying me from tip to toe. 'And who shall I say is asking for her? The President of America?' One thing I had learned during my time in Ireland was never to try and outwit a Dublin man – you'll fail miserably and look a bigger fool than you really are.

'Tell her it's Francis Scully. She'll know who it is.'

'Fine', he said, and putting his cap on his head he said, 'Wait here', before disappearing down a long flagged corridor. His metallic heels clipped the solid floor like a demented metronome.

As I waited in that voluminous atrium, imperious portraits of past surgeons stared down at me as if to say, 'Shake, quiver, bow down. You are in the presence of greatness'. I walked outside and sucked in great lungfuls of dank Dublin air to try and calm my nerves.

'She said she'd never heard of you, Mister.' The porter had returned, his face daring me to call his bluff. I was just about to toss the flowers in a nearby bin when Mary appeared.

'Don't believe a word this man says', she said, giving him a quick hug. 'He's the biggest mickey-taker this side of Galway Bay.' With that, she slipped her arm through mine and tossed a quick, 'See ya, Paddy', over her shoulder before looking at me and saying, 'What kept yer?'

I can't remember much of what we talked about that day or even where we went. I do remember walking along the banks of the Liffey and stopping every now and then to watch the colourful barges as they moved up and down on their way to and from the docks. I seem to remember that we watched the lock gates opening on the Royal Canal too but how we got there I have no idea. We talked, we sat, we looked, we watched, and then suddenly it was dark. It was the most memorable day of my life.

'I'd better leave you home, Mary', I spluttered suddenly as the church clock struck 7 pm. I looked at her, having no idea where she lived or even where we were at that moment. 'Where do you live?'

Mary shouted a sudden, 'Boo', at a cheeky seagull that had landed on the rail next to her in the hope of stealing some food. She watched the squawking bird as it flapped a few feet further along the rail where it landed and dared us to chase it further away. 'It's not the sort of area that respectable gentleman like yourself should visit, Frankie', she said airily. 'But they're a grand lot in their own way', she added, before continuing her assault on the seagull with another, louder, 'Boo!' The gull was not impressed.

My confused look must have weakened her resolve not to tell me, so linking her arm through mine she pulled me along the path saying, 'Come on then. If you promise to be good, then I'll look after yers.'

'Where are we going?' I asked, smiling at the fun of it all.

'Home to meet mi ma and mi da and mi sisters and mi brudders', she smiled guilefully.

'And where, may a respectable gentleman ask, does my dear Mary and her "brudders" live?'

'In the Liberties, Mista', she answered, laying on her Dublin accent thicker than butter!

We giggled like kids as we ran hand in hand along the streets. But the streets didn't laugh back. They became bleaker and blacker and the faces of those we passed mirrored the looks of the buildings they propped up. There were children everywhere, even at this late hour. Children with pinched features, children with rags for clothes, children too tired to lift themselves off the steps they sat on. And there was shouting, too. Shouting men, shouting women, men and women shouting at each other.

'Don't be worrying about all that', Mary said, and squeezed my hand in reassurance. 'It's how people talk to each other around here. Most of the menfolk are so thick in the head that you have to shout just to get their attention!' Her smile went some way towards comforting me, but it felt I was moving into a strange new world.

'Here we are', Mary said, and pulled me through an open doorway and up some step wooden stairs. The clack-clack of our feet worked better than any doorbell.

'Mary's home!' a high voice piped. 'And she's got some auld geezer with her!'

'You mind your manners, Eoin', Mary said with no trace of malice in her voice. 'This auld geezer as you called him has come all the way from America just to meet you!' Young Eoin's eyes opened wide with amazement. 'Jaysus', the boy said.

This was met with a soft cuff across the back of his head. 'Don't be taking the Lord's name in vain, young lad. Now go inside and have your tea. It's past bedtime for you.' The words were spoken by a slight woman who appeared to be an older sister of Mary. The eyes were the same, she sported the same carriage as Mary but as I came closer I noted that the flecks of grey in her dark hair suggested that perhaps she was older than she first appeared.

'Ma', Mary said, giving the woman a big hug. 'This is the kind man who looked after me when I got sick on the boat.' Turning to look at me she added, 'Ma, this is Frankie Scully.'

'Pleased to meet you Frankie Scully', the good lady said.

'Delighted to meet you too, Ma'am … Mrs Nash', I replied.

'You'd be welcome to come in and have a cup of tea if you'd like, Frankie', she said.

It was such a simple invitation, but it threw me into complete confusion. I must have muttered six 'Ah's and several 'Um's in the space of one sentence before they understood that I was offering my apologies and suggesting that I had to get home.

'I'll get Paddy to put you on the right path', Mrs Nash said. The words were unspoken but it was understood that an innocent abroad such as I could easily land in difficulties in the alleyways and badly lit streets of the Liberties. Paddy was a genial giant of a youth, who, after ritually ribbing his sister – who was several years his senior – led me out of that human rabbit warren.

'Ah, it's a tough place to live', he said as we walked along. 'But the people are grand really. No-one has two pennies to rub together but the sun still comes up each day.' He slowed, and only our footsteps made any noise in those dank streets. 'Well, maybe not the sun, but you can be certain that it will rain most days which is almost as good to a Dubliner. Saves having to wash the dust off the carriages we keep out the back for best!'

Paddy saw me as far as my road to Donnybrook then shook my hand and left. 'Great to meet you, Yankee!' he shouted back along the street. 'I'll tell mi sista that yer not as bad a lad as you look.' With that he disappeared into the black night.

'Have a nice day?' asked John later on as we listened to the chimes of 10 pm from the nearby church clock. We were sitting by his fire and the gas light hissed its yellowed light on his old features. I suppose the smile that creased my face in two must have given him a clue. 'Ah', he intoned as he reached for a pipe. 'Good. I'm glad. Was she as nice as you remembered?'

'Better', I grinned back. 'Far better.'

We both sat there quietly cocooned in our own memories. The hot embers of the coal fire blushed black with the cold draughts sucked in under the closed door in search of sustaining warmth. The hiss of the gas lamp and the flickering pageant of the fireplace was almost hypnotic.

'It's a great thing when you re-visit your memories and the reality is even better than you expected', John said as he suckled on his burnt-out pipe. 'But in my experience, it's the exception to the rule.'

I remained silent for the very real reason that I didn't want to let go of the scent of Mary that still lingered about me, and within me. I also had an inkling that John needed to tell me something. I had come to learn that the man was not only telling me stories of his time in Australia, but also giving me some lessons on how a man can live in the backwaters of life and still make a difference. Not a front-page-of-the-newspaper type experience, but experiences that touched others' lives and left a residue of goodness behind.

EIGHTEEN

Going forth…and back again

JOHN TOOK UP HIS STORY AGAIN.

'When I got back to Tipperary, I went straight home. To all intents and purposes it was as if I'd never left. Everything was exactly as it had been before I left – even the window boxes had the same flowers in them, pansies. Pansies are one of my favourite flowers. I think it's the impish face they project into the world and yet they are as fragile as gossamer, like a butterfly's wings. The oak front door, as stout as any portcullis, stood guard with its brass knocker burnished bright, by Matthew, no doubt. My father always had great faith in Matthew. "Sound man, that. Would have made a great sergeant major", he often said. The trouble was that Matthew was a proud supporter of Dan O'Connell, the Liberator, and I suspect a secret supporter of Wolfe Tone as well.

Dan the Liberator was a great man who did his best to bring some independence to dear old Ireland. The trouble, as he soon found out, was leading those poor blighters to freedom was like trying to herd cats! By the by, did you know he fought a duel in Oughterard? Strange coincidence that, because that's where I took up a Resident Magistrate position when I finally left the Swan River. I always wondered why they chose Oughterard, seeing as the D'Esterre fellow he was fighting was a member of the Dublin Corporation. It seems that our Dan had described Dublin Corporation as a "beggarly corporation", and seemingly Mr D'Esterre took severe umbrage to that. It was he who challenged our Dan to a duel. As things turned out, he should have kept his mouth shut because he lost … badly. Shot in the stomach. Dropped like a stone and died of his wounds, poor creature. They said he was a fine shot, too, but obviously not as good as Dan. But Dan was mightily upset by it all. Swore never to fire another shot in anger, and he kept his word, too. Just goes to show, eh? Even if you win and you lose your own self-respect in doing so, you lose in the long run.

'Now, where was I? Ah yes, Tipperary: Matthew. Nothing changes …

'I knocked and went in. Word was sent to Mother who was in her room. Needless to say she came down the stairs as nimbly as a little Colleen. She stopped in front of me as if to devour me with her eyes and then we embraced as only mother and son can. When I think back on it, that was the pinnacle of the whole visit. Seeing my mother looking so happy to see me … I still miss her.

'There was much fuss and noise made in those first couple of days. Big meals with the family were organised and eaten. Promises to visit and endless questions answered. Then it stopped. You see, everyone was busy with their own lives and my return was just another thread in the tapestry which was their daily lives.

'Life rumbled on in its well-oiled way in Tipperary and Dublin. I did meet with brother James and we discussed the proposed changes that our nephew John had put forward. It seemed like a grand plan. According to John, everyone would be better off, especially the farmers who were depositing their money with us. I even remember saying to James, "This seems just too good to be true." And in retrospect, it was. John was good at pulling the wool over people's eyes. It wasn't just us who were brought down by the man. When the crash came it produced a mighty mess all around Ireland, England and even Europe. But I'm getting ahead of myself again.

'At the time, I realised that I loved Ireland. It was in my blood. The green fields, the green hills, the little rivers with their red fin perch, bream and pike. The smell of turf smoke coming from the thatched cabin chimneys and the sound of cattle ripping the luscious grass from its roots. And the rain, of course. Once you've lived through an Australian summer you come to love the sound of steady rain on a tin roof. Bliss indeed.

'But back in 1838 it was as if life in Tipperary was going on around me and I didn't seem to be a part of it. If it hadn't been for Dr Burges, perhaps I would have eventually found myself a job and joined in the familiar rhythms of Irish life.

'Dr Burges worked his practice about twenty miles from Tipperary in a small town called Fethard. My father had got to know him as he travelled around the county on magistrates duty. The good doctor had sons in Australia, and Mother thought it would be nice for me to meet someone with a mutual interest in the country. God love the decent woman, little did she know that the lads were on the Swan River which is as far from Sydney town as Moscow is from Cork!

'Still, it was good of her. I suppose if she could have fore-seen what would happen after that dinner party, she might have invited the Bishop of Dublin instead!

'Dr Burges had three sons: William, Sam, and Lockier – named after himself. They'd gone out on the *Warrior* in 1830 and seemed to be doing very well out in the new colony. I'd heard of the Swan River Settlement from my talks with Father Brady in Windsor, and my good friend David. It seemed like it had a great future and yet I'd also heard that it was struggling to attract people to go and work there.

'"You should go there", Dr Burges said over dinner, fixing me with the tines of his fork. "Sam writes me that there's good pasture there and that the price of land is very reasonable." He returned to his thick slices of beef and in the short silence which followed I stole a glance at my parents to see what their reaction might be. There was none.

'"Did you say they've been there for eight years, Doctor?" my mother enquired. The rumble from his throat and the nod of his head as his cheeks bulged with food indicated that she was correct. "And have they ever come home in all that time?" she continued. I could detect in her voice a trace of longing. It's a tone that all mothers have for their sons when they are far away from home: they wish them every great success but they still want to see them and hold them to their bosom one more time.

'"No, Mrs Scully, they haven't", he said, resting his implements on the edge of his plate and sitting back in his chair. "May I congratulate you on a very fine table, Mrs Scully? That's the most tender beef that I've tasted in many a long month. And that gravy ... delicious." Touching the napkin to the corner of his mouth, he wiped his tongue around his teeth and then went on. "The boys keep in regular contact, although, as yet, there is no established postal connection between the young colony and London or Dublin. At present it goes via Batavia or the Cape, which is a bit problematic, but between the three of them I hear at least half-a-dozen times a year. If their mother had still been alive no doubt it would be more often and no doubt they would have come home in the meantime."

'He spoke the truth. I automatically looked at Mother and knew that if she were not here then I wouldn't have come home either. By the look in her eye I knew that she knew that too.

'"Tell me more about this settlement, Doctor", I said. "It sounds an intriguing place." So it was for the next little while the good doctor entertained us with stories of snakes and spiders, frogs and mosquitoes, kangaroo and emu and a sun that would blisters the skin off any insane Irishman who ever set foot upon its never-ending white sandy shores.

'I was hooked.

'The next day I met with my father in his office and told him of my intentions. He was a good father in many ways. He provided well for his family, he was much loved in the community and he was a good moral force helping to shape our future characters as young boys growing up into manhood. Not only that, he was an astute man of business, too. He knew that prospects back in Ireland were few and far between for young men like myself. It was usually down to one of the three professions: law, medicine or a man of the cloth. But he knew that at heart I was a man that valued his place in the community and, like himself, wished to be of service to his community.

'"You've made a tough decision, John", he said from behind his desk. "I grant you that there are great opportunities, but there's also great potential for a great loss of money, too." He played with the pencil in his hand, twiddling it through his fingers time and time again. "Whilst you were away in the army, I've actually given it a great deal of thought. The colonies are where our future lies. The Americas are really opening up now and people who aren't shy of hard work will do very well there. I believe the same is true for Australia. But it's still a very young country."

'He paused as if making a decision. "I'm happy to back you in your endeavour."

'I interrupted him, saying, "Thank you, Father", but he cut straight back.

'"Let me finish, please. As I said, I'm prepared to back you but you must be honest with me. You must stay sober and hardworking and keep me regularly informed as to how things progress. If things fail to thrive, then you must tell me so straight away. If something should happen to me, then I won't be able to vouch for you any longer. In other words, time is not your friend." He paused and looked me straight in the eye. "I may not be old yet, but I'm getting old and anything may happen. When I die, your mother will need you. If things are not settled in Australia then you must come home. Do you understand?"

'I nodded my head. "Thank you, Father. I will not let you down."

'"One more thing", he continued. "Take Helen with you. She's been fretting away ever since you left the nursery so you may as well take her. She's a tolerably good cook but most importantly, despite her looks, she's a strong woman and will serve you well."

'His offer made me a happy man. Helen was my favourite servant and she would spoil me rotten given half a decent chance. "I can't thank you enough, Father", I finished.

'"Then don't", said my father, standing up and extending his hand to shake mine. "Remember, stay in touch and be honest with yourself … and me!"

'What I would have given for a hug from the good man. But Father was not a hugging man. He was far more formal than that. As a result, I suspect that in my middle years I too never had the ability to show my feelings well. It makes for a lonely life, Frankie.

'Without saying anything he reached for his cheque book, filled out one of the slips and passed it across to me. "That should help you get started, son", was all he said.

'I read the figure, which, whilst it was a generous sum, would not make me a rich man. But it would allow me to buy stores and equipment, and most importantly, help buy some land when I got to the shores of Western Australia. I had my remittance money from the army which allowed me 150 pounds against buying land in the colony, but every extra pound meant an extra acre too.

'It was one of the last times that I saw my father on this earth.

'A week later, everything had been arranged and I headed to Liverpool with Helen in tow to arrange our passages. I intended to take the *Hindoo* which was to leave shortly. That left me just enough time to meet with my agent in Liverpool, whom I'd sent word to, to help secure me indentured help and to reserve a cabin for me. My farewells were not as poignant as on the first occasion when I'd left home, that was until I said goodbye to Matthew. I'd known him since I'd been a wee lad. He'd saved me from many a scrape over the years and we'd shared many a good laugh and the odd sly sip of poteen in the barn too. He was what you'd call a sound man. Yet when I came to shake hands with him along with the other servants, he had tears streaming down his cheeks. It shook me to my roots. I can see him standing there now, and when I remember that moment, the funny thing is that I feel like a young man again. What strange gifts memories can be.

'In Liverpool, I met the McPherson brothers who were to be my shepherds in Australia.

'Donald and John McPherson had been forced to leave their croft by the rapid changes that were sweeping through Scotland. Industrialisation and the advent of steam-driven engines and mills had pulled nearly all the young people into the burgeoning cities. There they hoped to find a better life and a steady income. But as the cities were thriving, the countryside was dying. For many like the McPherson boys, the option was emigration or starvation.

'They were hardy young men with granite for muscles and heads with canny, clever minds hidden under their highland bonnets. They were as different from me as day is from night, but I felt that they were men I could do business with. Once you'd got behind that dour, tough exterior they were as honest as the day is long. As well as the Scottish contingent, there were two more men whom my agent had indentured. They were fine lads too – Chapman and Cook. Not bad fellows for a couple of Englishmen!

'I signed all the relevant papers, gave instructions for my trunk to be taken on board and stood at the rail once more watching those hidden islands disappear into the murky mists.

'There were forty six passengers along with me on the *Hindoo*. I had a cabin towards the stern of the ship with a Major James Tait in the cabin next to mine. He also had an indentured servant with him, a strapping young fellow called John Sutton. Tait headed off for Mandurah, or was it Pinjarra? Any ways, it was well south of the settlement. He went into some sort of partnership with a couple of others and did very well for himself, I believe. Even became a justice of the peace, I hear. But on the boat he was a taciturn fellow, which suited me to a "T".

'The McPhersons boys and the two Englishmen travelled below with the other emigrants for the Swan River Settlement. Not that it makes any difference which deck you're on when you're on a small boat way out to sea, unless you're a total snob, which can make life intolerable for everyone. Helen managed as only Helen knows how. She seemed to be always on hand whenever I'd lost anything and had the uncanny knack of knowing what I wanted even before I'd realised I wanted it myself.

'"Didn't I rear you from a gosson", she'd say as she bustled about her business – or should I say, my business.

'The highlight of that particular trip was the Fairbairns. They'd arrived on board with their young daughter, Margaret – a sweet little thing. Her mother, Elizabeth, happened to be heavily pregnant when we set sail. When she went into labour I offered them the use of my cabin so that she could have a bit of privacy. Needless to say, Helen took charge of everything.

'"No place for a man here, Captain", she said, pushing me out of my own cabin.

'Young Isabella was born alive and well with a great set of sea lungs! There was one other lass there who gave Helen a hand. I seem to remember her name was Catherine Hart. She was very calm when the baby was born. A good woman with a grand, soft heart. I often saw her around Perth on my trips down there. She was indentured to one of the bigwigs in town but they treated her well. When her time was up, she moved on to South Australia with her niece. I never heard what happened to her after that.

'Apart from the happy arrival of young Isabella, the trip was fairly routine. By the end of the trip I was over a life at sea and was very glad when the gulls appeared. When the lookout called, "Land Ahoy", and we could just make out the tip of Rottnest Island, everyone on board let out a great cheer.

'Rottnest is a funny little island with some funny little creatures on it – they call them quokkas. They jump around like little kangaroos but they don't even come up to your knees. Friendly as a cat some of them: fearless, too, which was almost their undoing when we Europeans started to eat them! The Dutch, who'd arrived long before the English, thought they were rats, and that's why it was called "Rats-nest". The Dutch never had a great sense of humour, did they?

'Rottnest's a sweet little place to visit, it's away from the colony but a part of it as the same time. You can see the smoke coming from the settlement from the island harbour. Not that you'd go there now. They turned it into a prison for the natives. When you come to understand more about those natives then you begin to see what a living hell it was for them. To be taken away from their country for seven years for some minor offence and all the time their beloved land lies unreachable on the horizon. Believe me, the Irish may have had a tough time over the centuries with the British, but at least they didn't take our country from us.

'After we'd rounded Rottnest, we entered Gage Roads where our pilot met us. He directed us to a safe anchorage just offshore from Fremantle. Lighter-men appeared in their longboats and we were ferried ashore to where a scattering of little cottages made up that fledgling metropolis.

'Jumping from the bow of the boats, many of us waded ashore to the pristine white beach. Even though it was the end of April, there was still a warmth in the water and the sun shone like a burning orb in that massive dome of a blue sky. I fell in love with the place immediately. The recent rains had greened everything up as far as the eye could see – what wasn't there to love about the place? I couldn't wait to get started.

'Having supervised the unloading of my luggage and stores, I asked the McPhersons to look after it until I sent instructions from the main settlement as to where to take it.

'I found a boat that would take me upriver to where the new colony was really beginning to put down its roots. The journey was fascinating. It wound around high chalk cliffs on one side and low flat sand hills, covered with scrub, on the other. The water was salty all the way up and we gave a great "whoop" of delight when we saw a small pod of dolphins herding some fish for their morning feed. They are such grand and playful creatures. Who could not stop and wonder at the sight of them?

'Rounding the bend, the river opened up to the size of one vast lake and in the east lay a low line of hills on the distant horizon. The journey from Fremantle took us from the higgledy-piggledy conurbation that was the point of arrival for settlers and sailors, to the small, more orderly village which was home to the administrative centre of the new colony. By the shoreline I got my first sight of the famous black swans that sail imperiously along just as their albino cousins do in the northern hemisphere. I soon learned that the natives have their own lore how the swans ended up having black feathers and red beaks. It's one of their stories from their Dreamtime. In the local Noongar legend, swans were once white and had grey beaks; that was, until they made the mistake of boasting about how beautiful they were in front of the wedge-tailed eagles. These majestic raptors didn't take too kindly to such boasting and punished the swans by plucking their feathers out and leaving them to die in the desert.

'But the crows found the bruised, bloodied birds and took pity on them, covering the swans with their own black feathers so that the eagles could no longer recognise and attack them.

'The thing was that the swans still had a few white feathers left at the end of their wings to remind them of what they once looked like, and their beaks have been stained red ever since from the bloody attack on them by the eagles.

'The Noongar have some great bird stories, thankfully most of them aren't as bloody as that one. Remind me to tell you about the willie wagtail sometime!

'The settlement had a simple wooden landing area which was mainly deserted in the midday heat, so I headed up the incline to Mr Leeder's Hotel. It's a respectable inn situated on the main street just a short distance from where the Governor lives. There's a small enclave of government buildings there, including the courthouse with its silvery, shingled roof. Most people thought them to be rather severe looking structures, but I liked them. The military have their barracks opposite the Governor's place with a small detachment of the 63rd currently based there.

'The settlement itself is no bigger than a small village, even by Irish standards. It's such a pretty location with the river reaching to the foot of the hills that lie to the west. They call the biggest of those hills Mt Eliza. You'd have to laugh at the optimism of the locals though. Mt Eliza's no mountain; it's about a hundred foot high! But it's in a beautiful location, rising up over the river with thick bush scrub giving occasional glimpses of massive, white limestone cliffs and towering native trees which are home to cockatoos and sea eagles.

'It's a different kettle of fish when you look to the north of the settlement, which is as flat as a pancake with mosquito infested swamps and even worse – frogs! Talk about insomnia! Now, I'm a rural man myself, but the sound of those frogs at night would drive a man half crazy. And if they don't drive you up the wall then the mosquitoes finish the job with their insatiable blood lust and their high pitched "zzzz" which feels like they've taken up residence inside your ear. To every man and his dog, it was plain that if the place was to survive and expand, then they'd need to do something about those swamps. Either the frogs and mosquitoes had to go, or the humans would!'

NINETEEN

Difficult choices

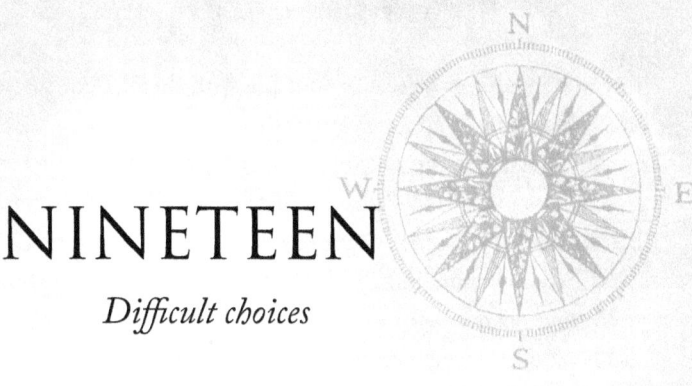

BY THEN IT WAS EARLY SUMMER AND THE evenings had lengthened considerably. John finished talking and we just sat there listening to the tick of 'that auld clock', as Maria called it. John saw me looking at it.

'A wedding present', he said quietly, 'from my brother Francis. He's a good lad, much like yourself. He's an MP in London and tries his best. Helped me when the whole Tipperary Bank business blew up and got me the Resident Magistrate job in Oughterard. The clock's a lot like him – steady, reliable, and always right!'

'When did you and Maria get married?' I asked him.

'1851.'

'Was there ever anyone in Australia who you thought you might marry?' I asked.

'That's a bold question to ask a happily married man, and his good wife upstairs in the marital bed.' There was no malice in his voice as he spoke.

'It's just that …' I struggled with the words that felt like a big lump of lead in my throat. 'It's just that, when you have really strong feelings for someone, your thoughts kind of turn towards spending the rest of your life with them', I blurted. I blushed at the sound of my own voice.

'Ah. Mary, is it?' he asked kindly, but there was a gleam of impishness in his voice. 'Love or lust?' he asked, reaching into his pocket for his pipe. 'Young people find it difficult to tell the difference sometimes, don't you think? Are you using your head, your heart or your –', and here he pointed with the stem of his pipe in the general direction of my crotch!

'I'm serious, John', I replied with ruffled pride. 'Mary's different. She makes me feel special and I think I make her feel special, too.' John said nothing. 'It's as if words aren't necessary when we're together, though she does like to talk a lot. But I think it's just nerves. I'd do just about anything for that girl.' The earnestness in my voice must have impressed John a little.

'And on that note young lad, I think it's time to sleep on it. Past my bedtime.' Rising to his feet he exaggerated a groan, saying, 'This getting old is not for sissies!' He stepped towards the spot where I had risen to bid his goodnight.

He hugged me, which was the first time he had done that. 'Listen to your heart, but think with your brain, son, and everything will turn out fine. Good night and God bless you.'

TWENTY

A new beginning

MY COURTSHIP WITH MARY WAS MAGICAL – that's the only word that can really describe it. Not that we had that much time together. She was busy with her work and family life and I was in transition from law to medicine.

Pa had changed his mind about cutting me off, as John had wisely foreseen. But the understanding was that I would only be given one chance and if that didn't work out, then I had to head home.

Thankfully, I loved what I saw in the College of Surgeons.

It was a time of great transition. The scientific and industrial changes of the last fifty years were now turning into a real force at every level of society, and that included the musty halls of medicine. They still wore frock coats, which were really quaint, but their thinking was beginning to change radically. No longer were things accepted at face value: everything was questioned.

Science was taking over.

Even so, some things do not change. At the most fundamental level, the anatomy of the human body was just the same.

Long gone were the times when anatomy was an abomination, although certain religious fanatics still believed all forms of human dissection to be a 'mortal sin'. Thankfully none of our teachers subscribed to that medieval way of thinking.

In the anatomy rooms I found both ends of my soul. At one end was trepidation and fear. At the other, wonder and awe. As students we spent a great deal of time coming to understand the mechanics of the body; all the time I had a vision in my mind of Leonardo's great works done all those centuries past. For me, the anatomy of the human body is an unbelievable masterpiece.

Even more mysterious was how the body worked at a microscopic level. With the recent advances in that area, a whole new science was developing and our understanding of who we really are got a whole lot more complicated. In whatever way you looked at it, our bodies were proving to be the real miracle of life on this great and wonderful earth.

I loved it. I couldn't get enough of it. When I'd catch up with Mary I was plain bursting with things to tell her, and she would sit there and just smile until her cheeks ached and she had to hug me to stop me talking.

But it wasn't all plain sailing with her. Some of her family were none too fond of having a Yankee cousin coming along to take her away from them. One of them even had the idea that he'd get my Mary married off to one of his friends. One day I bumped into him in one of my now rare forays into a public house. He was a bit the worse for wear from too much porter. When he saw me, he put down his pint, wiped his face with his sleeve and bored over towards me.

'You stay away from Mary', he slurred. 'You hear me? You stay away from her or yers'll have me to deal with, mister clever clogs.'

That must have been one of the shortest visits I made to a pub in all the time I spent in Dublin.

I was telling John about it later that evening. 'That's the trouble with passion', he said. 'It can get you into an awful lot of trouble – and most of it not of your own making!'

We were taking a constitutional along by the Dún Loagharie pier at the time. It was a glorious Irish summer's evening; even the gulls seem subdued by it. A few wealthy men's yachts were moored about fifty yards away and the sound of the ropes slapping the mast added an almost hypnotic effect to the scene.

He leaned against the stone wall and held his side. 'You OK, Uncle?' I asked in some concern.

'I'll be fine in a minute, lad', he replied when he got his breath back. 'The challenges of old age! What doesn't kill you makes you stronger – or so they say. I just need to walk at a slower pace and then I'm fine.' He gave me a reassuring look. 'Come on', he said. 'Let's go to the end and have a sit down there.'

When we got there, we sat and enjoyed the view of the sun slowly setting in the western sky.

'This is probably what I missed the most when I was in Australia. These long, slow evenings that seem to drift into night.' He chuckled to himself 'Down there', he indicated south with the stem of his unlit pipe, 'it's lights out and off to bed once the sun has set. But then you get a glorious night sky full of the most amazing stars. The Milky Way in Australia is just stunning. Mind you, the Noongar have a different way of seeing it. They don't actually see the stars, you know. They see the dark bits! In fact, if you look at the black bits of the Milky Way you'll see a dark emu! What's more, they work out the seasons by watching for when the emu appears in the sky! It's quite fascinating.'

He sucked on his pipe. 'Sorry lad, you were telling me about Mary and her interesting family. Do you have any serious intentions there?'

For all the age difference between us I really felt that John was a special friend now and I saw him as someone I could share my sincerest secrets with.

'I think this is the real deal, John', I replied. 'She's just amazing. I don't know where to begin to tell you about her, really.'

'You don't have to son. It's written all over your face!' He put his hand on mine and I can still remember how cold his fingers felt. 'Love and passion are very similar, and they also come with a fair dose of suffering too. So be prepared. Life, love, passion, suffering and hardship are all chapters in the same book.' He paused. 'That's what makes it all so wonderful. If she's the one, then you'll have to accept the full package, which includes brothers who threaten to take care of you. I remember an ex-convict in New South Wales telling me once: there are two powerful emotions on the planet – one is love, and the other, hate. Unfortunately, hate is much stronger, but love lasts much longer! Long may it last, eh, laddie?'

A chill breeze came up over the sea from England and we decided to head for home. Maria greeted us and said she'd left some supper on the table in the front parlour; she was off to get some beauty sleep. John kissed her on the cheek and I followed suit. 'Don't let him keep you up to all hours, Frankie. That man could talk a stone into submission!'

Once we'd settled into our chairs and armed ourselves with a generous glass of Irish whiskey, John took his first sip and took up his story again.

TWENTY-ONE

Toodyay

'WHEN I AWOKE THE FOLLOWING DAY I sought out Mr Leeder to ask him where I should buy my supplies. William Leeder was a good man, if a little over-fond of his own produce! Originally he was from the east of England, Suffolk I believe, and for a man in his mid-forties, he looked a little flushed in the face and what we in Ireland would call prosperous lookin'. He was honest and generous with everyone, whether they were the Governor or the tap boy, and I admired him for that. Strange to report that he was a shoemaker originally, but then everyone who arrived at the settlement had to turn their hands to things that weren't natural for them.

'Mr Leeder suggested that I talk with Lionel Samuels, who was the biggest trader in town. There was a Mr Mangles too, but William didn't hold too much trust in him for some reason. Samuels turned out to have been in the colony for about ten years. He was Jewish by religion but race or creed never stood in his way if there was business to be done. He was a bright man, too. An Oxford man at that. But his heart was in his business. He'd try anything to advance himself, just as any farmer would do anything to improve his lands or his flocks. I heard once that he would say, "Honesty is not the best policy, it's the only policy." I liked the cut of the man, too.

'But first I needed to find some land away from the town.

'I'd been intrigued by the stories of Dr Burges of where his sons had settled out towards York. With that in mind I went to the Colonial Office and asked to see what maps they had and what lands were available to lease. The building was easy to spot as it sported the first public clock in the colony, the timepiece having only been fully commissioned within the last few days!

'I selected three blocks on a site at a place called Mt Bakewell in York, a place on the far side of the hills over in the east of the settlement. The 150 pounds from my remission ticket, which I got when I'd resigned my commission, came in mighty handy when it came to pay for it. This was to be my base whilst I looked around to see how things stood there. The next day, along with Cook, Chapman, the McPherson boys and dear, loyal Helen, we set out for York.

'That last night before we set out, I heard of a Tom Yule, a big man with a big heart, who had a big bush selection out at a place he called Byeen. He was a widower with a daughter back in England. He also had another place nearer the Swan River, much closer to the settlement and which would seem to better suit his more sociable activities. He had taken a shine to the daughter of the doctor out there – Lucy Harris.

'A colourful character was our Tom. He was involved in a duel once. More accurately he was second to a man called Johnston who fought the only duel in Western Australia, against a man called Clarke. Tom was on the losing side that time! Clarke was charged with murder but needless to say he was acquitted by his so-called peers. Not that that worried Tom at all.

'When we arrived in town, he was looking for someone to look after the land out at Byeen, otherwise he'd lose it. The word was that he'd been trying to get someone to lease it so that they could run sheep on it to improve the area. He was even offering to throw some extra land in to sweeten the bargain, too. I was told that he'd been looking for someone to take up the offer for a couple of years, but with no luck.

'It certainly gave me something to think about as I pulled on my boots the next morning.

'Things in the settlement at that time had been slowing down, not that it had ever been hectic there. There were only about 700 settlers in Perth itself. Where we were heading – York – was even tinier. Most new arrivals continued to head to New South Wales, and even though they arrived by sea, the settlers, traders and military heading in that direction would stop at Albany, over 300miles away on the south coast. Very few people ever came via Perth. Our little Swan River Settlement was still a speck on the western shores with great talk of potential, but the reality was it was still struggling to survive.

'Only forty babies had been born in the previous year and a steady stream of workers were draining the colony of its lifeblood, heading east in search of a better life. And who could blame them? Trade was virtually non-existent: there were no ships, and few buyers. Exports were mainly done on speculation when a ship arrived and needed cargo to take back to the old country. There was only one guaranteed direct ship to the old country, and that was around Christmas each year when long-awaited mail and parcels arrived and the wool clip was packed off. Back then, there were no guarantees of anything.

'But it still attracted those who were willing to take a risk, not that all of those risks were particularly well-thought through! Lieutenant Grey was a case that rapidly comes to mind. Shortly after we arrived he returned from his blighted expedition to the lands far north of the settlement. In my estimation, he was, how can I put it politely, somewhat arrogant! But his trip from way up north, on foot with no supplies, counts as a major feat of endurance in anyone's language and gave the colony something to talk about for months afterwards.

'He'd set off on an American whaler with a small support group and a Noongar guide called Kaiber. But the two long boats they attempted to reach shore with were wrecked up at Gantheaume Bay about 300 miles north of Perth. I have the man's journal here somewhere.'

John searched along his shelves and pulled out a couple of volumes of leather bound journals. '*Journals of Expeditions of Discovery*', he read slowly. 'It's the second one we need.' Thumbing through the pages, he read extracts at random.

> 'After I had for some time looked round on this scene I returned to the party and received the report of the carpenters, who, having examined the boats, stated their inability to render either of them fit for sea. To this I had already made up my mind; and even if the boats had been uninjured I doubt whether we could ever have got them off again through the tremendous surf which was breaking on this part of the shore; whilst to have moved them to any distance would, in our present weak and enfeebled state, have been utterly impossible.

'No resource was now left to us but to endeavour to reach Perth by walking; yet when I looked at the sickly faces of some of the party and saw their wasted forms I much doubted if they retained strength to execute such a task; but they themselves were in high spirits and talked of the undertaking as a mere trifle.

'I gave them all warning of the many difficulties they had yet to encounter, and did this not with the intention of damping their ardour but in the hope of inducing them to abandon some portion of the loads they intended to carry. I entrusted a small pocket chronometer to Mr Walker, and another to corporals Coles and Auger; and to Ruston I gave charge of a pocket-sextant which belonged to the Surveyor-General at Perth. Coles and Auger also undertook to carry a large sextant, turnabout; all my own papers, such charts as I thought necessary, and some smaller instruments I bore myself; but Kaiber, in order to relieve me, took charge of my gun and some other articles. Mr Smith carried his sketchbook and box of colours. I ought here to state that, in all the difficulties which beset those individuals to whom I entrusted anything, they never, except on one occasion, and by my orders, abandoned it: indeed I do not believe that there is a stronger instance of fidelity and perseverance than was evinced by some of the party in retaining, under every difficulty, possession of that which they had promised to preserve for me.

'It goes on a bit about the countryside, etcetera, etcetera.

'I now entreated the men to disencumber themselves of a portion of the loads which they were attempting to carry. Urged by a miscalculating desire of gain, when the boats were abandoned they had laid hands upon canvas and what else they thought would sell at Perth, and some of them appeared to be resolved rather to risk their lives than the booty they were bending under. The more tractable threw away the articles I told them to get rid of.

'But neither entreaties nor menaces prevailed with the others. The tenacity with which they clung to a worthless property, even at the risk of their lives, is almost incredible, and it is to be borne in mind that this property was not their own, but what they had taken from the wreck of the boats. Did I even induce one to throw anything away another avaricious fellow would pick it up; and their thoughts and conversation, instead of running upon making the best of their way home and saving their lives, consisted in conjectures as to what they would realise from their ill-gotten and embarrassing booty.

'Da-di da-di-da ... he goes on about meeting more natives, some of them apparently fairly grumpy ones. But as he had a rifle the white man rules again!' John leafed through the pages. 'More about the landscape, naming places after friends and important people. Ya di ya ... oh, here.

'Yet it was quite manifest from recent events that the majority of the party had not only made up their minds not to accelerate their movements, but had fully resolved to compel me to pursue their system of short marches and long halts. Being fully aware of the danger which threatened them, it remained for me to act with that decision which circumstances appeared to require, and to proceed by rapid and forced marches to Perth, whence assistance could be sent out to the remainder. For this purpose it was necessary that all those who accompanied me should be good walkers and resolute men; for if any accident happened to the portion of the party I took with me, arising either from want of energy, want of discipline, or any other causes, that portion of the party which remained behind would have been reduced to the last extremity.

'Having formed this resolution, it became necessary to make a selection of those who were to accompany me. In determining however upon this point I had but little difficulty; for it was evident that those men who during our late toils had shown themselves the most capable of enduring hardships, privations, and the fatigue of long and rapid marches, were those who were the best suited for the service I now destined them for. The following was the division I made of the party: I named:

'Corporal Auger, Corporal Coles, H. Woods, W. Hackney, Kaiber, the native, as those who were to accompany me, and left the remainder under the command of Mr Walker. The party I left, and who were not required to proceed by forced marches, consisted of:

'Mr Walker, Mr Smith, Thomas Ruston, C. Woods, T. Stiles, A. Clotworthy.

'More rivers named, a couple of hills for his friends. Ha: a rat eats half the remaining damper he has in his bag ...

'The men, who had a little flour left, boiled two tablespoonfuls of this in about a pint and a half of water, thus making what they called soup. In the meantime Kaiber came in and told me that he had found some holes in which the natives had, according to their custom, buried a store of By-yu nuts (the nut of the Zamia tree) and he at the same time requested permission to steal them.

'I reflected for some time on his proposal; I was reluctant to mark the first approach of civilised man to this country of a savage race by an unprovoked act of pillage and robbery; yet we were now in the desert, on the point of perishing for want of food, the pangs of hunger gnawing us even in our very sleep, and with the means of temporary relief at hand. I asked myself if I should be acting justly or humanely by the others, whose lives were at stake if I allowed them to pass by the store, which seemed providentially offered to us, without pointing it out.

'In my perplexity I turned to Kaiber: his answer was, "If we take all, this people will be angered greatly; they will say, 'What thief has stolen here: track his footsteps, spear him through the heart; wherefore has he stolen our hidden food?' But if we take what is buried in one hole they will say, 'Hungry people have been here; they were very empty, and now their bellies are full; they may be sorcerers; now they will not eat us as we sleep'."

"Good, it is good, Kaiber", I replied; "come with me and we will rob one hole." And accordingly we went and took the contents of one, leaving three others undisturbed. I brought back these nuts to the men and we shared them amongst us.

'Took a bit of sense from a so-called savage to knock some sense into his head. Long list of dry rivers, barren land and the great sufferings that thirst can cause. I can identify with that lad …

'As long as they remained on the banks of this river bed a glimmering of hope remained; but I felt convinced from the general appearance of the country that there was not the slightest probability of our finding water there, and resolved therefore still to continue a direct route. When I gave this order the weak-minded quailed before it: they would rather have perished in wandering up and down those arid and inhospitable banks than have made a great effort and have torn themselves away from the vain and delusive hopes this watercourse held out to them.

'We had marched for about an hour and a quarter and in this time had only made two miles, when we suddenly arrived upon the edge of a dried-up bed of a sedgy swamp, which lay in the centre of a small plain, where we saw the foot-mark of a native imprinted on the sand, and again our hearts beat with hope, for this sign appeared to announce that we were once more entering the regions of animal life. We soon found that another part of the swamp was thickly marked with the footsteps of women and children; and as no water-baskets were scattered about no doubt could exist but that we were in the vicinity of water. We soon discovered several native wells dug in the bed of the swamp; but these were all dry, and I began again to fear that I was disappointed, when Kaiber suddenly started up from a thick bed of reeds and made me a sign which was unobserved by the others, as was evidently his intention.

'I hurried up and found him with his head buried in a small hole of moist mud, for I can call it nothing else. I very deliberately raised Kaiber by the hair, as all expostulations to him were useless, and then called up the others.

'Kaiber had completely swelled himself out with this thick muddy liquid, and from the mark upon the sides of the hole had evidently consumed more than half of the total supply. I first of all took some of this moist mud in my mouth, but finding a difficulty in swallowing it, as it was so thick, I strained a portion through a handkerchief. We had thirsted with an intense and burning thirst for three days and two nights, during the greater portion of which time we had been taking violent exercise under a fierce sun. To conceive the delight of the men when they arrived at this little hole of mud would be difficult. Each, as he came up and cast his wearied limbs on the ground beside the hole, uttered these words: "Thank God"; and then greedily swallowed a few mouthfuls of the liquid mud, protesting that it was the most delicious water and had a peculiar flavour which rendered it far superior to any other he had ever tasted.

'Shoots a cockatoo, eats it. Finds some fresh water mussels, eats them. Buckets down with rain and they nearly freeze to death.

'As soon however as it was light enough to see our way we started, and moved slowly onwards in a south by east direction. The men were all completely crippled from the cold of the night, and it was with the greatest difficulty I could get either them or the native to move. My own energies were however only raised from these calls upon them, and I cheered them on as well as I could. Corporal Coles, my faithful and tried companion in all my wanderings, could scarcely crawl along. The flesh was completely torn away from one of his heels, and the irritation caused by this had produced a large swelling in the groin. Nothing but his own strong fortitude, aided by the encouragement given him by myself and his comrades, could have made him move under his great agony.

'Still however we advanced slowly; other lives depended on our exertions; and whenever I reminded the men of this for a minute or two they quickened their pace. Pale, wasted, and weak, we still crawled onwards in the straight line for Perth, which I assured them they would reach on Saturday night or Sunday morning.

'Getting closer to Perth … meets some natives.

'The natives no sooner heard the gun and saw me approaching than they came running to me. Presently, Kaiber called out to me, "Mr Grey, Mr Grey, *nadjoo watto, nginnee yalga nginnow*", "Mr Grey, Mr Grey, I am going to them; you sit here a little"; and he then, with his long thin ungainly legs, bounded by me like a deer. "Imbat, friend", I heard him cry out, as a young man came running up to him. I grew giddy; I knew Imbat by name, and felt assured that at all events the lives of a great portion of my party were safe. In a few minutes Kaiber had given an outline of our adventures and present state. Fearing such mischances as had really happened to me, I had, previously to my departure to the north, done my utmost to cultivate the friendship of the northern natives; and most of them, even to the distance of sixty or seventy miles from Perth in that direction, had received presents from me. My name was well-known amongst them as a tried friend, although indeed my common denomination was "W'okeley brudder", or Oakley's brother; for, from my giving them flour, they concluded that I was a relation of the baker of that name at Perth.

'My anxiety for those I had left behind me now increased, and about an hour and a half before daylight I started for Perth with Imbat, leaving the others to follow as rapidly as they could, and telling them that I would have food ready for them at Williams's cottage, who was the settler living farthest north from Perth. In about an hour and a half I reached Williams's hut, which I entered, and found his wife and another woman at breakfast.

'I had often got a drink of milk at this cottage when I had before been at Perth, and I flattered myself that Mrs Williams would recollect me; little calculating how strangely want and suffering had changed my appearance. The two women only stared with the utmost surprise and said, "Why, Magic, what's the matter with you?" (They alluded to a crazy Malay who used to visit the outsettler's houses, and who had somehow or the other acquired the nickname of Magic.) I was rather hurt at my reception and said, "I am not Magic"; at this they both burst into a roar of laughter and Mrs Williams said, "Well, then, my

good man, who are you?" "One who is almost starved",
was my reply…

'I now washed and made myself as clean as possible. I could obtain no conveyance to take us on to
Perth and therefore started to walk in with Imbat,
leaving the others to complete their breakfast; but I
soon found myself dreadfully ill from having eaten
too profusely; still I pushed on as well as I could, and
in about an hour and a half reached the house of my
friend, L. Samson, Esquire. He could not believe it was
me whom he beheld, but having convinced himself
of the fact he made me swallow about a tea-spoon-
ful of brandy, and, recruited by this, I was sufficiently
recovered to wait upon His Excellency the Governor
in order to have immediate steps taken to send off a
party in search of my missing comrades.

'Now how's that for a bit of daring do, eh? It just
gives you an idea of how tough it is our there in the
bush. Strong men will die without water and even if
they find water they need discipline, too. You never
think of that when you set out on what you believe
is an exciting adventure. That Australian outback is a
cruel mistress!

'But back to the story I began.

'We were young. Our backs were strong and the
world was full of promise.

'Before we left, I'd made the decision to secure the
lease of land from Tom Yule, but first I had to secure
my land in York. So we headed off eastward with a
Whadjuk Noongar whose family lived in the hills
area. He was a shy man called Bilya. He spoke broken
English and as we walked along I began to pick up a

few words of his language. I asked how it was for his people when the white settlers had arrived.

'"Not good for us mista', he replied simply, and walked on in silence.

'I knew of the massacres that had occurred in the east and felt ashamed of the cruelty of those who had slaughtered innocent women and children. My father had taught me that we're all equal under God, the trouble being that many of those in authority firmly believed that these so-called savages were not even on the scale of equality. But not all.

'"I've heard of a man called Yagan", I said after about half a mile of listening to the cart wheels and the occasional squawk of a white cockatoo. Bilya's stride didn't alter although he darted a quick look in my direction.

'"Bad story mista", he said.

'"Tel' me about him. No rush. We've got all day", I said in a weak attempt at humour.

'"Yagan", he began. "He was the son of Midgegooroo. Their country over there." He pointed with his stick in a south-easterly direction. "Know what Yagan said about your mob? 'You came to our country; you have driven us from our haunts, and disturbed us in our occupations: as we walk in our country we are fired upon by the white men; why should the white men treat us so?' That's why they killed 'im. Some of you blokes spoke though. Mr Lyon, 'im good bugger, he said Yagan a hero."

'I remember reading later on in the *Perth Gazette* that Lyon believed that Yagan and the Noongar people, who were being arrested for the "crimes" against settlers, shouldn't be regarded as criminal or outlaws, but as prisoners of war. I'm inclined to side with him. In my view, they were just defending their land and property.

'Yagan was finally shot. When his body was recovered, his back was skinned to obtain his tribal markings. He was decapitated and his head was smoked and taken to England as a memento of the "Swan River chieftain".

'Skinned, decapitated and his head smoked! Makes you wonder who were the real savages were.'

TWENTY-TWO

York

'ON MY WAY TO YORK I WAS IN HALF A MIND to check out Tom Yule's place at the Byeen, but thought better about it and set our course for Mt Bakewell. The fact was that Tom's place was twenty miles north of a small place called Toodyay, which itself was another twenty miles north of York. When you're walking through dense, prickly scrub with no path to follow, that extra forty miles can seem like 100.

'As we walked I had plenty of time to think about what I'd learned in the short time I was at the settlement. Tom had called his place Byeen, even though the area itself was known as Bolgart. It was said that the word comes from the Noongar for magic and spring water, or the word for a star. Interestingly enough, it was also the name the natives used for Yagan when he met with George Moore! Now there were two men from different cultures and who yet had so much in common!

'We were heading into winter and the rivers and creeks could be treacherous at that time of year. The last thing any of us wanted to happen was to lose all our supplies and have to go back to Perth – even if we could. I had some money left over, but the truth of the matter was that there was very little stock back in Perth, and it could be months before any arrived from overseas.

'I'd also agreed to deliver some letters to the Burges brothers from their father. Having lived in the colonies before, I knew how precious those things were.

'Coming down from the hills that divide the Perth basin from the rest of Australia, rolling green hills stretched out before us to the far and distant horizon. Fingers of smoke from isolated settlers' cottages evaporated into the blue sky and birds screeched at one another. Every now and then a willie wagtail, or chitty-chitty as the natives called them, would land and cockily gyrate close to us. They were cheeky little fellas. Cheeky and friendly but as fearless as Finn McCool himself. I've seen them take on birds ten times their size – even eagles. Mighty little fellas those.

'As we came down from the dividing hills, we stopped where Ensign Dale first sighted York. The lad was only about twenty at the time. When we first gazed upon it, York comprised just a few houses, a couple of barns, an army barracks with some outhouses which was home to eight soldiers and about 100 acres of cleared land spreading out from the base of the hill. Standing on the rocky hill top looking down at the deep green of the trees that lined the Avon River, I can really understand why Dale named it after his native Yorkshire. There'd been rain in the night which had left the air cool and clear. Now the sun had come up and every bush, blackboy and tree sparkled like it had diamonds in it, and every cobweb was like the most beautiful tiara any princess ever wore. There was no water left on the surface as the ground had soaked it all up. The air was so *fresh*. All I wanted to do was suck great lungfuls of it into me and feast my eyes on the amazing new countryside that stretched out into the distance.

'We found Tipperary, the homestead of the Burges brothers, out along the river and were met by Sam. He was about the same age as me and, according to the local gossip, enjoyed the bachelor life to the full – sometimes a bit too full if you ask my opinion. The older brother was William. He was more serious and driven, if you get my drift. Lockyer was the one with itchy feet. He and William scouted the land as far north as Geraldton, a couple of hundred miles away to the north. Good men. Sound men and they did a great job for York.

'When I took on the Toodyay job later on, I was too far away from them to get to know them much better, but when I did call they showed me great hospitality. We also had one thing in common – I suppose all Irishmen do: horses. They had a small race track on their property and the annual York show was an event I never missed in all my years there. Now that really was fun!

'The land I'd selected was next to the little town site. It was flat land and not far from the river. Mt Bakewell, another of those mighty midgets, was a few miles distant but was a great place for picnics, not that we had much time for picnics in those early times. After a couple of days we'd pegged out the land, made a clearing and set up camp. Helen gave it a womanly touch with a few native flowers that she'd found God-knows-where.

'It was good land and ideal for sheep, and we'd decided that if the seasons were good to me, we'd put some wheat in, too. Europe needed wool and I was determined to give them as much as I could produce. Even more pressing, though, was the fact that we all needed bread to eat! The soil itself, where it wasn't rocky, was a rich loam very different to the sand found back near the coast. I truly believed that we could get some decent crops off it with hard work and determination.

'Over the next few months we established the Scully land and brought in some sheep. I must admit, buying those first sheep used up more of my resources than I had anticipated. The cost of wethers and lambs were almost prohibitive but if we could hold on for a couple of years then I knew we'd be alright.

'Once we were established, I left the younger McPherson to look after the place, and went up to Bolgart with the others to see what the situation was like there. Travelling at that time of year was no hardship. The winter rains had greened everything and the creeks and rivers were full but not wild. We stopped briefly in Toodyay and spent a nice evening with the Drummonds of Hawthornden.

'James Senior was a fine botanist who'd had a colourful history in the colony. The man left a great legacy. His botanical streak had obviously rubbed off on his son Johnston, because the two of them were forever off foraging for specimens whenever they could. Next in line was James, who was my age and a sound man. We got along well. The youngest of the brood, John, had been a bit of a wild young man in his early years but he settled when he joined the police force. As a consequence of his statutory duties, he spent a great deal of time travelling around with the natives, learning their language and getting to understand their customs.

'John didn't abandon all the ways of his youth and some of his choices certainly raised eyebrows back at the main settlement. You have to understand that for most of us bachelors, the company of white women was almost unheard of, mainly because there weren't any reputable single ladies available. For

John, that was not too much of an issue. I'm afraid he took advantage of the native women, which nearly led to his undoing and proved a mighty tragedy for young Johnston, too.

'The Drummonds were generous and genial hosts. Many's the evening we passed in each other's company when our work caused our paths to cross.

'Next day we were up early. The Drummonds had warned me that the land would become flatter the further north we went and that there were a few marshy areas around. I'm glad they told us that because we almost bogged the cart on a couple of occasions. As my mother used to say, forewarned is forearmed.

'It was a grand day for travelling and after several miles we found the Bolgart springs. First impressions were certainly very encouraging. Everywhere was green and the grass was head high. Mind you, the flies had teeth and the mosquitoes were maddening. We decided not to camp by the springs but to head west. We negotiated the marshy area until we found the Tom Yules lease at the Byeen. It was easy to find because there's a balancing rock by a spring, which the local Noongar say has magical influences.

'Tom might have enjoyed the high life back in the settlement, but he'd hardly scratched the surface out on his land. In fact, he hadn't made any improvements at all, which meant that we'd need to get a move on if we were to be ready in time to receive our sheep, or to plant some crops in a month or so.

'Tom had a massive lease but when we looked at the land he'd offered me, I could see that it wouldn't suit. The biggest drawback was lack of any water on our section. From the maps, I knew that there was almost 200 acres of land closer to Bolgart which hadn't been taken yet. So I took the gamble of setting up camp on that block. Later on I would have to head back to the main settlement to register it in my name and purchase it outright.

'First up we had to clear a site for our buildings. We called the area Victoria Springs in honour of our great Queen back in the old country. I heard after that my predecessor as Resident Magistrate in Toodyay, Captain Whitfield, had informed the Governor Stirling that, "Captain Scully I believe has settled himself on government land adjoining the grant of Messrs Houghton and Lows and not on their grant as originally intended." Those men were Tom Yule's partners in the land-buying business. We may have settled in splendid isolation, but the jungle drums beat loud and distant even in that part of the world!

'Now the real work began. We marked out the area for the house: a simple structure, which was to comprise a bedroom and a parlour. Next we measured out the area for the kitchen, storeroom and servants quarters. This proved to be far bigger than we'd anticipated. In fact, it was over forty foot long and sixteen feet wide. I can tell you, it was hard work putting it all together. Hard, hot work. We had to fell trees, split them into slabs, saw them into shape and then fill the holes with clay to keep out as many feral creatures as we could. The windows were covered with hessian and the roof thatched in the old style using a thatch made from the blackboy bushes which abounded everywhere.

'That blackboy tree is a marvel. They have a thick black stump of a trunk with a mass of stiff green fronds for a top. When a breeze blows through those fronds they can mesmerise you with the lightness of their dance. The Noongar call them Balga trees – not that they're renowned for their height, but perhaps more so for the passage of time it takes for them to grow just one inch! It takes a decade for them to grow just one foot, but the natives use every part of it for something or other. The dry parts, which are to be found underneath the thatch, they use for kindling even in winter when everywhere else is wet. Then there's the gum which they extract and mix with kangaroo droppings and charcoal to make a paste. It's the best glue I have ever used anywhere. Dries as hard as a rock. And of course, the grass fronds which make for as good a thatch as you'd find anywhere in Ireland.

'Those trees are different from anything you ever saw. Sometimes the trunk will split into one, two, three or four thick stems. I heard a funny story about Balga trees once. A poor, innocent young lad from the settlement was told to take a message out to a family who lived up near Guildford. He was told to go a mile past the town until he came to a two headed blackboy and then turn left. Well, the poor lad was in fear of his life all the way there until he understood the directions. He often used to tell the story against himself. It's funny how language and laws turn on the definition of a word!

'We worked hard in those first few months and made good progress. Then, as the season moved on, with the warmer weather came the flies. Enough flies to drive the whole of Ireland mad – and all of them seemingly on Tom Yules property. They sure pestered the life out of us. We quickly learned how to cut holes in old flour sacks to cover our heads with. We must have looked like Ribbonmen from way back!

'And the ants: the Lord save and protect us, they had to be seen to be believed! Not the little tiddlers you find on a honey pot. These monsters were big enough to lift the honey pot and twist open the lid if they wanted to. Like the flies, they didn't attend to your discomfort in ones and twos, they came on in battalions. A million mandibles to munch on soft Irish flesh. I hated those black devils. And another great pain was walking into spider webs. They're strong enough to catch a swan! And always in the back of your mind was, "Where's the spider now?"– You'd know if you'd seen the size of them …!

'Every new arrival is regaled with stories of wild life in the bush, and you know what, they're all true! Other stories I heard proved to be the product of fertile imaginations and rank discrimination, especially the ones that said that the so-called savages were not to be trusted. Those rumours had become entrenched thanks to such eminent men as Governor Stirling who, in the past, had warned the York settlers to have no dealings with Aboriginal people. He wrote to them. "Impress on every European the necessity there is by keeping arms in working order." That had the wonderful effect of making a certain settler called Heal set his dogs on a group of female Balladong Noongar, forcing them to take refuge in the deep water of a waterhole that once been theirs!

'These people weren't savages. They had an ancient code of conduct and a spirituality that allowed them to survive in Australia for over 40,000 years. They had their rules and regulations, and spearing a person in some part of their anatomy to settle a score had been standard retribution for them for longer than we Europeans had been wearing long pants for. So when the Balladong Noongar heard what had happened to their women folk, they took their retribution on Mr Heal. It was all looking pretty messy with men on both sides wanting to pick a fight. But John Drummond organised a *"waangkiny-iny"* – a get-together to talk – with the Balladong mob and things were settled peaceably.

'Unfortunately, my eminent predecessor, Captain Whitfield – he who passed messages on about me to the Governor – overlooked the fact that a settlement had been reached and arrested the two Noongars. One of them ended up dying of injuries he received along the way back to the main settlement, and the other ended up being hung.

'Beggars belief, doesn't it?

'All of this was known back in London, of course. I've read the reports from back then. Their understanding of the situation appeared most enlightened. One particular report I read from the British House of Commons about the rights of Aboriginal people before the law, debated, "Should district magistrates be allowed to issue summary punishments?" as was happening in Western Australia. "Should Aborigines have the power to appear in court? Could they be represented by Counsel? Have they rights to an interpreter?" Another report I read was by the Buxton Select Committee on Native Peoples, which ruled that within the recollections of many living men, "every part of this territory was the undisputed property of the Aborigines". It came to a conclusion about when the "Territorial rights of the natives were considered … whether as sovereigns or as proprietors of the soil, [they] have been utterly disregarded. The land has been taken from them without the assertion of any title other than that of superior force."

'After Stirling had gone, things began to change.

'The new man, Hutt, arrived and he immediately set about enacting structures to help the poor displaced people. Yet like all perfect intentions, they were administered by sometimes less-than-perfect people. Some of his choices were, how can I say this, a little stiff under the collar! I had the misfortune to run up against one of them, Mr Barrow, Protector of Aborigines. Looking back I suppose I may have over-reacted, but then I ask myself, was he doing his job properly?

'By the way lad, if you think I'm waffling on too much you must tell me.'

'No, go on, Uncle', I replied.

'Now where was I? Ah yes, we'd been warned to be on the lookout for any troublemakers. Needless to say, we never had any. I did report some stolen sheep a few years later, but the man was a recidivist and no worse than some white settlers or soldiers. Not that there were a lot of Noongar in the area any more. The numbers had been falling since the settlers had arrived. If you'd read the papers in England you think that we colonials were either shooting them, or killing them off with the diseases we brought with us! Grog took its toll of course. But smallpox was just as lethal. That should never have happened! As the whole civilised world knew, that new vaccine of Mr Pasteur's was in use everywhere and was given to all the white people in the colony. But not the black fellas! But it wasn't just smallpox that killed. Influenza, when it came through didn't really worry if you were white, black or khaki coloured: it killed every creed and colour.

'Out there at Bogart we soon slipped into a routine. Not only did we have to establish our own place, we had to run sheep on Tom's property and build a hut to conform with the lease agreement. That meant clearing land, ploughing the land, seeding it and stocking the land with animals. In winter we did as much clearing and ploughing as we could. It was mighty hard work. The land out there is fierce hard on the plough shares. It took me three days to plough two and a quarter acres. Most people could be self-sufficient on three and a half acres so I suppose that wasn't too bad for three days' work. In fact, no-one planted more than twenty acres anywhere in the colony! The simple fact was that there was nowhere to store it and nowhere to export it to in those early years.

'It was a tough routine. We were getting up about three, four or five in the morning depending on the weather. Then we set to at either clearing some more land, ploughing what we'd just cleared or keeping the well pure – and that was a job in itself. Helen did a monumental job keeping us all fed with limited supplies. We shot some kangaroo for meat and she made damper and sweet cakes to go with it. Believe you me, after a morning sweating it out in the field they tasted delicious! The only thing that stood between us and starvation was if we got a crop in and grew enough corn to keep us independent.

'We were blessed, as it turned out. We had good rains at the right time and as a result managed to get a decent yield from that first sowing. Bringing in the crop meant more hard work. The heat and the flies made it purgatory on wheels. The Noongar helpers we had secured laughed at us as we were constantly driven half mad by the flies, despite our best efforts at protecting our faces.

'Did I mention ticks? Another scourge in the bush. Big ones and small ones – they call the big ones kangaroo ticks, and there are salt and pepper ones, little black ones. It doesn't matter which one gets stuck into you, if you don't get them out right they'll itch like the very furies for weeks on end. Some settlers complained they got a rash after a tick bite, and others claimed they got sick afterwards but the doctor just seemed to think they were malingering! The settlers, not the ticks.

'Threshing is a slow process. Looking back, I don't know how we did it before steam engines arrived. Those mechanical behemoths managed to reduce a three week job to just three days. Once we had the grain in, we took it to Drummond's Mill in Toodyay, much to the great relief of our aching bodies. It just so happened that the Drummonds also brewed a particularly fine beer, which was much appreciated and helped to wash down the wheat and barley dust as well as slaking our seemingly unquenchable thirsts.

'We were a young and enthusiastic bunch out there in the bush but the regime we operated under was old, and slow to adapt. During my time there we came up with several ingenious ways of promoting the colony such as creating new trade routes, improving the roads, the docks, the ships and so on, but they all cost money. The last thing the government in London wanted to do was to spend one penny unless the mother country was certain of receiving the benefits. That's why, even though our flocks and crops grew, we were constantly hamstrung by lack of funds, lack of markets, lack of a decent transportation system, but most of all, lack of available cheap labour.

'I suppose if we'd treated the Noongar as equals and worked on treaties with them, they might have become our willing partners. But I say that with the benefit of hindsight. At the time, the white man was the boss and the savage was stateless, and now we'd made them landless.'

TWENTY-THREE

Captain John Scully RM

'ON 15 OCTOBER 15 1840, JUST A YEAR AFTER I'd arrived, the following announcement appeared in the colony, in the *Government Gazette*. "John Scully Esq. (settled at Bolgart) was appointed Resident Magistrate of the Toodyay District, on the resignation of Francis Whitfield Esq."

'It was a bittersweet appointment. Sweet, because with the appointment came £100 per annum to cover expenses of a horse, travel and various other expenses. Bitter, because the circumstances were tragic to say the least!

'Captain Whitfield – he who was the close correspondent with the former Governor Stirling – had, prior to coming to the Swan River, served in the Napoleonic wars before retiring to Ireland to live. This turned out to be just a brief respite from service to his country. He was offered land in the new colony and went out to the Swan to take up land close to the settlement in an area known as the Helena Valley. I can't remember why he left there, but he did, and moved up to Toodyay in 1836. I believe that he was one of the first settlers in the region. I know for certain that he was the first Resident Magistrate because I succeeded him. But then the poor man had to resign under the most extraordinary circumstances.

'One of his servants, Jane Green, an emigrant girl from the Orphans' Friends Society, fell pregnant at the age of 16. Naturally, there was a huge uproar as word spread like bushfire throughout the settlement. The real tragedy though was that the baby died and she was charged with the murder of her newborn infant. They had to get the government Resident Magistrate from York to take over the case. As a result of his deliberations the lass was sentenced to the Quarter Sessions where she was found guilty of the lesser charge of concealing a birth and sentenced to two years' imprisonment on Rottnest Island.

'Needless to say, the gossip brigade had a ball with the whole thing. Who the father of the unfortunate innocent was became frequently discussed behind many a fluttering fan in the weeks afterwards. Seeing as she was indentured to the only white man in the district, many a perfidious mind soon calculated that one and one made three!

'Poor Whitfield was completely ostracised and had to resign. His wife left him and moved into a place in the main settlement. That didn't stop the rumour mongers who whispered that perhaps Whitfield wasn't the real father of the child after all and that he was covering for one of his sons.

'To make his disastrous situation even worse, Whitfield had also made himself unpopular with the Governor by demanding that the Colonial Secretary provide a military force up at Toodyay! And no ex-army upstart tells Her Majesty's Colonial Secretary what to do! A lesson I was to learn myself when I asked for the exact same thing less than a year later!

'My friends in the area told me that Captain Whitfield lived until 1857 and he still has family ties in the Toodyay area. Just goes to show, time is a great healer. Oh, and by the way, the young girl as the centre of the saga, Jane Green, is now a grandmother and from what I'm told I think will outlive us all!

'Needless to say, even though the circumstances of my appointment could have been better, I was still mighty pleased with my new position. The major drawback was that I'd have to spend a lot of time travelling back and forth from Toodyay to Bolgart. The upside was that I had great workers back at Bolgart. Helen was an absolute brick in good times and bad. The McPhersons were men of steel with an eye to their own future and Cook and Collins were as reliable as the day is long.

'And I enjoyed the travel. It allowed me to stay with my new acquaintances and get to know them better. Being all men of roughly the same age, and many of them from Ireland, we had some great times. The races at York were a must, and St Patrick's Day called for a great deal of singing and carousing, usually ending up with me singing Irish ballads in the wee small hours of the morning. That's when we all missed home the most. Not that we missed the hangovers that came the next morning!

'The tyranny of distance and the lack of transport had its advantages and disadvantages. Being the Resident Magistrate gave me a certain prestige and power, but it didn't always make me the most popular man in the area! Sometimes I made myself decidedly unpopular by ordering people to come to me, usually for official business like petty sessions. When it came to assessing the improvement of landholders and the like, there was no alternative but to spend many hours in the saddle, which is hot, hard work. Even so, at the end of the day the social life certainly made up for all the physical inconveniences.

'About that time I received another appointment and found my name in the press once more. It was 3 December 1840, in *Inquirer Perth*.

> 'Resident Magistrate John Scully was authorised by the Bank of Western Australia in Perth to collect and forward monies as savings bank deposits from mechanics and labouring classes.

'And again on 5 December of the same year:

> 'John Scully (Resident Magistrate for Toodyay), Frederick Slade and James Drummond Jnr. were appointed for the ensuing year to carry out the provisions of the act of Council, to provide for the construction and management of roads and other internal communications, for the district of Toodyay.

'Yes, I remember it word for word! Getting funding for the road out to Toodyay was like pulling teeth. It was a great idea and there was no doubt that improvements were urgently needed. The sad fact was that there wasn't a spare brass farthing in the government coffers to pay for it. So most of the year the road was a dug up, sandy pit. In the wet season it turned into a dug up, muddy quagmire. That's if the flooded creeks hadn't actually washed it away altogether.

'According to the regulations, there were supposed to be four meetings a year. I'm not proud to admit that I found the meetings tedious. Over the five years I was on the board, I must admit to only attending two meetings – and one of them had to be abandoned as there weren't enough people present to make up a quorum! Maybe that's why the roads stayed in such a bad condition. *Mea culpa, mea maxima culpa*!

'They also made me the registrar of births, marriages and deaths at the end of January in 1841 – not an onerous position but it did save local farmers from having to traipse all the way to Tom Yule in Guildford to record the aforementioned events.

'The life of a Resident Magistrate wasn't so much difficult as it was time consuming, so I had to rely on my workers in Bolgart to keep things moving along. A routine was soon established. We thrashed our meagre harvest, had it ground and stored away; the flocks were sent out to graze to the west of Bolgart under McPherson's care and Helen kept the home fires burning.

'During one of the quieter spells, James Drummond suggested we take an expedition together to see what the lands to the north really looked like and to find which rivers drained into the nearby Avon from there. His father, James Senior, was more interested in the plants and trees than anything else, but James Junior, like myself, wanted to know if the land could support large flocks of sheep.

'In our party was Sam Phillips, the "Squire of Toodyay". Sam was a good man, over six feet tall and bearded to his chest. He had an abrupt manner and a quick temper to match, but they were offset by his kindness to children. He was the worst of us for a practical joke, a fact that could prove most aggravating when out on an expedition. You always had to check your swag before you retired just in case anything had been left inside it! But when you visited him at Culham, his homestead in Toodyay, he was a most generous host. He was a man for the horses, too and was a great rider. None of us could match him in a race across country – the man was fearless on a four-legged beast.

'We took a couple of native Yued people with us as guides and they were sound fellows, too. They knew where the water holes were and helped bring specimens to Mr Drummond so that he could review and record them.

'I've a couple of reports on the excursion, which found its way into the press. Protocol dictated that I inform the Colonial Secretary about all such ventures as all the lands we crossed were outside Crown lands. Hence the need to let them back in London know.

'I have to say the whole thing was a wonderful experience. Being the first European to walk in those areas was a delight and an honour. What appeared to be wide open spaces to the European eye, was a totally different landscape to the native one!

'The Noongar people have their own unseen boundaries and borders. It could be a clump of bushes, or an outcrop of rock, or more usually a dried-up creek bed. If you cross those invisible boundaries, believe you me, the "mob" whose country you enter will know about it soon enough. Before you know it, they'll appear out of nowhere to see whether your intentions are peaceful or not. In that respect, they're just like white people – but they carry spears with them, not guns!

'Here's the report which I've kept of that first adventure. It's from the local newspaper of the time.'

John handed me a sepia-coloured newspaper clipping from the Perth *Inquirer* dated 10 March 1841.

His Excellency the Governor has been pleased to direct
the publication of the following particulars of a recent
excursion from the Toodyay country to Moore River,
made by Capt. Scully, Messrs Phillips, Drummond,
and J. Drummond, with two natives:

The party started from 'Yerrindine' springs about
sunset on the 7th ult.; arrived at a spring called 'Byen'
in 3½ miles, halted for the night at 'Yulgeen' spring,
the intervening country having been found undulating, partly white gum forest, but mostly grassy hills,
resembling the land in the Toodyay District. Next
day the party proceeded about 10 miles NNW to
'Yenart', a springy tea-tree swamp, around which was
abundance of green grass, even at this dry period of
the year, and a considerable extent of land having
water within 2ft. of the surface. Between Yulgern
and Yenart, the country was generally level, sandy,
white gum forest, and produced much of the plant
supposed to be poisonous to live stock. Two miles
beyond Yenart they entered upon extensive grassy
plains, drained in the winter season by a brook which
is tributary to Moore River, and received the name
of Fletcher's Brook when discovered by the Surveyor-General in November, 1836. Following its dry
bed in a NNW. direction, in 8 miles more a pool of
fresh water was discovered in it called by the natives
'Cungin Cunginwing' – which appeared to be within
a month of drying up. Five miles beyond this brought
the party to a pool called Girdine, in Moore River,
where the water was excellent, and likely to be per-
manent throughout the year. The country watered

by these two streams is described as beautiful, open, and grassy, and much resembling that in the vicinity of the Avon and Toodyay. The soil is a bright sandy loam, and the grassy flats which extend from the river, vary from one to two, and sometimes more than three miles; the hills which skirt them being also covered with grass to their very summits. It was computed that within the limits visited on this occasion, there was abundance of grass for 20 or 30,000 sheep. On the grassy lands there are no grass trees – the species which Mr Drummond distinguishes as having leaves so tough that cattle and sheep do not eat them. The trees were observed to be the same as those which grow in the Avon district.

Returning that evening to Cungin Cunginwing, the party proceeded next day over open grassy country to 'Marramenip', a pool in the Moore, about five miles to the north. Here they fell in with a party of natives who informed them this was the first year within their knowledge that this pool had dried up; they, however, led on to a spring of good water 3 miles in a south direction, where the scenery is described as 'really beautiful, and, as far as could be seen in every direction, the country was open, undulating, and grassy'. The party then returned to Toodyay by their outward route, highly gratified with their excursion, and were given to understand, by their native companions, that the Moore was tributary to the Swan about 10 miles above Mr Shaw's estate of 'Belvoir'.

The result of this brief exploration in search of fresh stock-runs has proved highly satisfactory, as not only confirming previous favourable reports on the nature of the country about Fletcher Brook and the Moore River, but from its having made the Colonists acquainted with an additional tract of excellent land, within a convenient distance of the settled districts, and, probably, leading to more extensive pastures of the same description still farther to the north.

By His Excellency's command,
PETER BROUN

Colonial Secretary's Office, Perth John spoke only when I'd finished reading. 'Those were exciting times. Stepping into places where no white man had been before, now that was an adventure, my lad. Almost as good as falling in love, eh?' he said with a wink.

TWENTY-FOUR

Changing times

I WAS SITTING IN THE RUSSELL HOTEL IN Stephens Green reading the newspaper. John was due to join me as I hadn't seen him for some weeks. I'd moved out of Anglesea Road and in with some fellow medical students who had digs near Merrion Square. It wasn't that I minded the walk from John's home; it was the weather I had to walk in! Besides, I taken to medicine like a duck takes to water and for some reason the discipline that was imposed on us students was exactly what I needed at that time of my life.

'Reminds me of being in the army', John had said, 'and look how I turned out!' He wasn't a man to make jokes, and there was a tinge of sadness in his voice when he'd said it.

I was sharing with a fellow American and an Australian. He was all things that John had described about Australians. Whilst ninety-nine percent of students tended to treat the master surgeons with awe and enormous respect, Lockie had even been heard to address one of them by his Christian name – unheard of in those times. The surgeon was apparently so shocked he replied to Lockie using *his* first name. Needless to say, none of the rest of us had the intestinal fortitude to do the same thing.

One thing we all had in common was that we wanted to be there in Dublin, and we wanted to succeed. These guys knew how to party and have fun, but they had brains as sharp as scalpels and no-one took shortcuts when it came to studying hard.

John came in and I stood to greet him. 'What do you think of this, John?' I asked, pointing to a small article buried on the third page of the *Irish Times*. 'A guy back home called Edison reckons he's created an electric light bulb. Imagine that. A light created by electricity. Just think what that could mean.' My own mind had been buzzing since I'd read about the invention.

The good man smiled and said, 'The world is rapidly changing, Frankie. I can just imagine what my old friend Rosendo Salvado will do when he hears the news! He'll light up his mission in New Norcia with the biggest lightbulb of all!' He smiled at his own attempt at humour. 'I hear he was over here talking to the gentlemen at All Hallows, drumming up support for his mission in Australia.'

The waitress came and took our order. 'Strange choice for a medical student', John muttered sotto voice.

'What?' I answered, unsure of where this might be leading.

He looked around the newly decorated room of the Russell Hotel. 'Meeting in a temperance hotel?'

'Seemed a reasonable idea to someone who's become acquainted with the pathological effects of alcohol', I replied in as professional manner as I could summon. We then both burst out laughing. 'It seemed a good place to meet and I hear the food's great, too!' I added more soberly.

'So tell me, lad, how is the blood and gore business going?'

'Sir, I am just loving it. It still blows me away how it all works so beautifully and yet it's just so doggone complicated at the same time. We've been using microscopes recently and the stuff you can see would make your eyeballs pop!' I felt myself getting excited just talking about it.

'So I take it you're enjoying it then', he grinned back at me. 'Tell me now, how's Mary? I though the two of you would have been calling on us. Maria misses feeding you. You know how women get about feeding young men.'

I felt a wave of guilt rise into my throat. 'Oops', I said. 'I'm sorry, John, but time just seems to get away from me when I'm at the college. You know, there's just so much to learn about each part of the body and scientists are learning more all the time.' I paused and straightened the knife and fork which were on the bleached white table cloth in front of me. 'Anyhows, I haven't seen Mary for a few weeks. She's had to go to Longford. Seems her grandpa has been taken mighty ill and her gran needs help to cope with it all. Her brother came to tell me – you remember me telling you about him?'

'He was the one who was asking after your health, I believe', John said, with a flicker of a smile on his face.

'The very one, John. But you know what? Without any porter in him, he's an OK guy. His name's John, too. I reckon he even likes me, not that he'd ever admit to that. Anyhow, Mary and I write each other, which is good.'

'When did you last hear from her?' John inquired.

'Today. I got a letter just after I'd posted mine to her.'

'You write often?'

'About every day', I said in honest innocence.

He eyed me with his rheumy eyes. He looked older than when I'd seen him last time. I noticed a tiny fleck of blood on one of the small sores that he had around his temples. He'd said they were sun spots from his time in Australia: 'Everyone's got them', he'd said.

'When you love something enough, you have to learn patience', he said. 'But the hardest thing to discover is that sometimes patience isn't enough and you have to let go of your dream.'

'One thing I can tell you, John, is that I'll never let go of the dream of marrying Mary', I replied sharply.

'I know son', he replied. 'I wasn't referring to you and Mary. I was thinking about something completely different. By the way, have you heard from your father recently?'

The simple answer was yes, but the complicated one was that Pa had written to me and once again had managed to rub me up the wrong way. He had ranted on about how much it was costing him to pay for me to become a sore-bones, what good was that going to be for the family business and when was I coming home to pay back on his investment in me! All he thought about was money and expanding his empire. John, on the other hand, seemed more like the father every young man dreams of and I'd come to love him deeply – Maria too.

'Yes, Sir, I have', I answered. 'He's well, the family are well and he sends his regards to your and Aunt Maria.'

'Ah!' He spoke the word as if he'd just opened the bag of Perseus and discovered a galaxy of mysteries! John scratched around to find his beloved pipe, something that I had come to understand heralded an imminent insight from the dear man. 'As a matter of fact, I had a letter from him too.'

Now that surprised me! 'Families are strange beasts, and the relationships between father and son can be the most dangerous beast of them all. Even though we weren't blessed with children ourselves, I still had a father.' His eyes twinkled more out of reassurance than happiness. 'Did your father talk to you much about when he was young?' The question was light but the answer was fraught with pitfalls.

'Not much, John. Pa wasn't that sort of man. He always seemed to be driven by making money and increasing his empire. Fuzzy family times were anathema to him. Not that he ever meant us ill, I think, more that he always seemed distracted by business. We just didn't seem to figure too much in his life apart from helping him build up his fortune.'

'Ah.' That word again! 'Did he never talk of his time in Ireland before he left for America?'

'No, Sir.'

John eyed me intensely. 'This isn't an interrogation, Frankie. I'm just wanting to find out how much you know and how much you don't know. Perhaps if you knew him better you might understand why he acts the way he does. Did you ever hear tell of your Aunt Polly?'

'No, Sir, I don't believe I did.' Why was I calling him Sir again? Something about the direction this conversation was taking seemed to disturb a dark place in my soul.

'Your ma and her sister Polly came to Ireland on holiday together when they were in their late teens. They stayed down in Tipperary with the family. They were grand and delightful beauties, the two of them. Your ma was the elder of the two. But it was Polly who your father fell in love with, even though your ma secretly loved him from the moment she set eyes on him. Maria could tell straight away that it was going to end in tears, but what could we do but watch and wait and be there to pick up the pieces when the inevitable happened.'

'But the inevitable didn't happen. Your pa and Polly were so joyously happy together. Everywhere they went the sun seemed to shine and even the rain seemed to feel softer when they were around. Then Polly died. It was a total accident and there was no-one to blame. They were out riding and her horse shied. She broke her neck in the fall and died in your pa's arms. The poor man was shattered. Your Ma was almost as broken hearted as he was and the two of them sheltered in the deep shadow of their shared grief.'

'I suppose that's was brought them close to each other. The common cause of suffering and despair. When she went back to America they wrote to each other. Your father was a restless spirit after that. Ireland had no hold for him anymore. He became a bit reckless, too. He drank too much and rode like seven devils were chasing him. It was as if he had a death wish. I suppose that life didn't hold too much for him. Then, out of the blue, he decided to head off to America and start a new life there. The rest you know.'

My brain, which delighted at absorbing facts about the human body and the rapidly changing face of science, was stunned into stillness by what it had just heard. It seemed that my vision of life was being challenged and changed on an almost daily basis. Then slowly, a new dawn arose in my understanding and in the light of that new day I saw a familiar figure: my father.

TWENTY-FIVE

Newspaper clippings

'TIME'S CATCHING UP WITH ME, FRANKIE', John said to me a few months later. He'd arrived at my lodgings with the old box that I'd seen in his store shed at the bottom of the garden. Despite its journey across town, it had managed to retain the smell of musty grass clippings and creosote.

'I've kept these since I was in Australia and I don't know what to do with them. I really don't want to burn them or throw them away. Too many memories. Besides, someone may find them interesting in the future. If I'd had children I would have burdened them with them it all.' He paused, looking at the brown box speckled with age and mould. 'Would you be interested in them?'

'Why, I'd be honoured, Sir', I replied instantly. I'd really come to appreciate John's confidences about the past and it all seemed so strange and different from either back home or Dublin. 'And if Mary and I were ever to have children, believe me, we're going to call one of them John Wyse in honour of you, Sir.'

Age had made the man more emotional, and tears formed in those old eyes of his. 'Thanks for the sentiment, Frankie', he said, and, reaching out a free hand, he shook mine with his bony grip. 'I can't stop', he said. 'Maria isn't the best today. Rheumatics. It's the weather.' Pulling his collar up around his scrawny neck, he turned and left.

Later that evening when I'd finished all my classes and the other lads had retired to their various recreational pastimes – the public house, the nearest ceilidh, or the latest girlfriend – I lifted the box down onto my lap and opened it.

John was certainly a very organised man! I leafed through the pages which he'd spoken of in the past until I reached the place where he'd left off his story.

The year was 1841 and I found a police report submitted by the local policemen in John's district of Toodyay, dated 20 July.

> His Excellency the Governor is pleased to direct the publication of a copy of the journal of proceedings of the Police force in the York and Toodyay District during the past month.
>
> By His Excellency's command,
> PETER BROUN
> JOURNAL OF PROCEEDINGS
>
> June 1st, 1841 OF THE POLICE FORCE IN THE YORK AND TOODYAY DISTRICT
>
> 1st – Patrolled to Toodyay
>
> 4th – Returned
>
> 2nd – Patrolled to Beverley
>
> 3rd – Returned

It seemed there was a deal of patrolling and returning! The report continued.

9th – Went to Beverley to endeavour to ascertain the names of the natives concerned in an attempt to rob Mr Parker of Avondale.

10th – Returned

11th – One policeman employed in serving summons

13th – It being reported that some natives had attempted to murder Mr N. Shaw, at his farm in the Toodyay District, accompanied by the Police I repaired to the place to inquire into the circumstances.

On my way received a letter from Capt. Scully, the Resident of the District, which confirmed the report. On my arrival at Capt. Scully's he gave me a warrant for the apprehension of the offenders.

15th – I despatched a native named Boonon to ascertain the course the natives had taken; having instructed him how to act in the event of his falling in with them.

16th – I proceeded with my party, accompanied by Mr Phillips, a magistrate of the District, to the northward, to intercept them in case they were taking that direction.

20th – Returned; and on my arrival at Capt. Scully's, he informed me that one of the offenders was in the employ of a settler in the Northam District, to which I proceeded, but found it was not the case.

22nd – Returned to Toodyay and found that, during my absence, Boonon (the native employed by me) had returned with intelligence (which he communicated to Mr Phillips) that the offending natives were to sleep that night a short distance from that gentleman's residence – and that night I fortunately succeeded in securing them.

23rd – Escorted them to Guildford; and on the 24th handed them over to the Guildford constables.

24th – Patrolled to Beverley

25th – Returned

28th – Patrolled to Toodyay

I was intrigued by the story and wondered what had happened to Mr Shaw or indeed the natives that had been arrested. As it happened, I needn't have wondered too much as John had neatly affixed the following report to the back of the police records.

QUARTER SESSIONS

Perth, July 1, 1841.

Before W. H. Mackie, Esq., Chairman, and a Bench of Magistrates.

The Chairman, in addressing the grand jury, congratulated them that so few cases had to be submitted to their notice, and that only one of the prisoners indicted formed a part of our own population.

The only case of importance was that of the three natives, Bob, Juleba, and Pingerry, who were indicted, the first for cutting Mr N. Shaw with an axe with intent to murder, and the two others with aiding and assisting therein. The particulars of the case are already fully known to the public, and the charge being proved on the evidence of Mr Shaw, and of Mr Armstrong, they were all three found guilty, and sentences of death was recorded against them. They will therefore be sent to Rottnest for the term of their natural lives. Mr Shaw interceded for the natives, and recommended them to mercy, stating that although Bob had struck the blow, he considered nevertheless he was indebted to him for his life, inasmuch as a party had come down with the intention of spearing him, which Bob had prevented, by engaging to wound him in the manner he had done.

Such a strange story. Spearing, retribution and the clash between two cultures. I knew from several stories that my uncle had told me that there was ongoing friction between the natives and the settlers. But the Noongar didn't give up that easily. They and their dogs continued to harass the flocks and live by their tribal rules of payback. And yet … and yet, great friendships were created between the possessors and the dispossessed John had told me that George Moore had been reduced to tears when his aboriginal friend Winmaar was speared in a payback by a mob of Aborigines from up near the Moore River.

I picked up a couple of pieces of faded newsprint:

> 17th August 1841 Created Justice of the Peace along with several others in the colony

> 20th October 1841 Created Resident Magistrate of Toodyay after the resignation of Captain Whitfield.

Seems like although he'd only been there for 18 months, Uncle John was rising rapidly through the ranks, as they say. It appeared that everyone who was appointed to a position of power was either a retired member of the military or a lawyer. A lot of them were Irish, too, which I thought strange at first, but then I realised that they were mainly from the Protestant ascendancy which still had a powerful say on that side of the continent.

But it wasn't all about politics and power, even in that tiny settlement. They were young men who'd come out to make their fortunes and for nearly all of them that meant farming. The money was, as they say, on the sheep's backs, as well as in the sandalwood and the growing of staples such as wheat and potatoes. They'd also learned that growing grapes and olives produced crops of similar quality to any of the best places in Europe. But there was one big hurdle they hadn't overcome: the chronic challenge of supply, demand and competition.

And, as is always the fact in new enterprises, there were un-expected challenges too.

November 1841

NEARLY all the persons employed on the farms of J. Phillips, Esq., and Captain Scully, in the Toodyay District, have suffered from an attack of illness, the cause of which appears to baffle at present the experi-ence of our medical gentlemen. Of course, rumour is administering to the tastes of the credulous, and the simultaneous effect of the disease, is attributed to the prevalence of some epidemic. We are well informed this is an erroneous impression, the symptoms being pronounced directly opposite to those which are apparent in cases of such nature.

I knew from my medical studies that diseases such as diph-theria, measles and whooping cough were constantly sweep-ing through communities and killing off the most vulnerable. Then there was smallpox, influenza and tuberculosis, all of which the Aboriginals had never been exposed to in the past. It killed them in droves. But John told me that these people were used to extreme hardship and sufferings. They were very familiar with the challenges of life and the imminent threat of death. They might not have built one lasting building, yet they had developed a spiritual legacy which was as rich as anything that he'd ever come across.

He'd told me some of the stories about their mythical figures and the Dreamtime stories which had evolved over many millennia. The one that sticks in my memory was the one about the Wagel.

The Wagel is their sacred serpent and lays its eggs at a place they call Goonininup, and which the settlers called Mt Eliza. It's that small hill John had told me about which overlooks the Swan River near the main settlement. To the Whadjuk Noongar it was a sacred site, but to the settlers with an eye to the future, it was prime real estate. Naturally, the natives had to go!

The Noongar were moved to a 'mission station' out at Jane Brook run by a Mr Abrahams. John told me that eleven of the twenty-three sent to the station died of influenza. Naturally, it didn't come as a big surprise that the other Noongar didn't want to send their kids there. According to the papers, there were other reasons why they didn't want to go there. Abrahams's place was also the first place where Aborigines were recorded to contact syphilis and tuberculosis.

I put the papers down and stared out through the window. My mind drifted to what I'd seen here in dirty old Dublin. It seemed like the only difference between here and there is the weather, because all of those diseases were staple infections of the Dubliners too!

As I read on, I learned there was another scourge that affected every settler — man, woman and child – and that was money, or more accurately the lack of it.

Money was short in the Swan River and investors in far-off London (whose memories were still fresh from the disastrous investment in the Peel district settlement) were not keen to put more money into a place with no obvious sign of good capital return. If they wanted to invest in Australia, for most of those wealthy men in their clubs in smoggy London, Sydney and the east coast seemed a far juicier fruit to pluck. But even there, recession was biting hard.

Uncle John seemed undaunted in those early years. He joined everything that he could in his efforts to improve the colony and his own situation, too. He was strong, he was healthy, he had his own land and he was carving a role for himself in the fledgling community. Yet at heart John was still an Irishman and like all Irishmen who had a good Catholic mother, John's respect for the Roman Church was deeply ingrained. Truth be told, he missed the rites and rituals of the Mass. With more and more of his countrymen and women trickling into the colony, he saw the need for a priest to organise things, and to act as a counter-balance to the sometimes bigoted Protestant hierarchy that ran the settlement.

I found a copy of the letter sent by a Mr D'Arcy to the bishop in Sydney asking for a priest, to which John was a signatory.

Perth, Dec 12, 1841

My Lord,

We beg to call your attention to the following facts. In this and the surrounding towns there are to be found all kind of Protestant ministers who show a good deal of activity in preaching their creed. There are to be found two of them in Perth, one in Fremantle, one in Guildford, and in almost every district of the colony. Not only do they try the conversion of the natives but also endeavour to bring to their churches some of our Catholic flock. Hence the difficulty for a Roman Catholic to persevere in his faith, many a one having already fallen away and joined one or other of the Protestant creeds. Should a favourable opportunity present itself they would, we believe, come back to their faith. To us Catholics our greatest, and I dare say, our only joy would be to be able to build a church and to have a priest sent us whom, we promise, we would support to the best of our means.

Trusting that your Lordship will take this important matter into consideration, and that you will provide in all kindness for the salvation of our souls.

We remain,
Your Lordship's most devoted servants,
ROBERT D'ARCY

Robert D'Arcy was head of a committee of five amongst whose names was to be found that of Captain John Scully RM, Toodyay!

It just shows that the man had many facets to his character: a man of faith and a man who loved horses, too. From a Yankee perspective that seemed like a mighty fine balanced outlook on life!

TWENTY-SIX

Gamekeeper or poacher?

SITTING ON THE OBSERVATION PLATFORM watching a surgeon remove an infected arm is a million miles from understanding what it was like to deal with a man whose leg had been speared by a native – even though the outcome might be the same. From where I was sitting with my chin cupped in my hand, arm resting on the rail in front of me, everything seemed under control. The surgeon spoke with consummate authority, even though it was very likely the patient would die of sepsis. The tiled harlequin floor spoke of solid scientific foundations and the wood-panelled walls exuded ages of accumulated wisdom.

All knowledge had led to this moment. Everything had a place and everything was in the right place. Then I thought of what John must have experienced.

He'd lived in a time and place where ancient man met modern man. Where custom and ritual clashed with law and order. Where lines drawn on a map were more real to governments than the people who lived on those boundless lands. It was a place where the government Resident Magistrate was torn between two worlds – one as a frontiersman, and the other as an 'up-keeper of the law'. It was a grey area and one where I suspect Uncle John had managed to 'live between the lines'.

To the European, it all came down to the definition of what a squatter was and who owned the land. The assumption being, as always, that the Noongar and other Aboriginal clan groups across Australia had no land rights whatsoever!

John had been running his sheep on the Yule property, but with the winter rains, the opportunity of greener pastures was almost irresistible. He wasn't alone there. The Drummonds had been with him on his expedition to the north of Bolgart along with Sam Phillips, and they knew what was out there! They were the ones who'd discovered the vast tracts of land that Uncle John had called Victoria Plains. These lands were all beyond so-called Crown land, and to those in the know, they were just asking to run sheep on them. James Drummond Senior, the botanist, had marked out the areas that were contaminated by the poisonous weed which killed imported cattle and sheep. It was an irresistible fruit waiting to be plucked. The locals knew that as they were so far from the Colonial Secretary's office, so there was a good chance that they could get away with it. But it seemed that someone must have whispered into the ear of the Governor, because around that time, Governor Hutt instigated a debate on a Bill to prevent the unauthorised occupation of Crown lands. And guess who got a special invite to attend?

I'd read a clipping the previous night:

July 21st 1842

LEGISLATIVE COUNCIL, Council Chamber, Perth

That previous to the commencement of the adjourned debate on the bill to prevent the unauthorised occupation of Crown lands, on the next meeting, Capt. Scully may be examined before the committee of the Council upon the subject of the operation on the system of squatting in New South Wales, its probable effects in this colony, and generally upon the subject of the said bill; and That Capt. Scully, Mr Bland. Mr J. W. Hardy, Major Nairn, and Mr J. Drummond, be requested to attend at the bar of this Council for that purpose.

I hadn't read what John had said and was imagining what his story might be when I was shaken from my reverie by the surgeon asking, 'Scully, what is the blood supply to the femur? I'm about to chop this man's leg off and I don't want him to bleed to death. Any suggestions?'

Later that night after I'd finished study, I sat with a modest glass of whiskey and in the light of a gas lamp took out the report of Uncle John's reply.

July 28 1842

LEGISLATIVE COUNCIL –
EVIDENCE ON THE SQUATTING BILL

Capt. Scully, of Toodyay, examined

I was about 15 months in New South Wales in the years 1837 and 1838. I was in the army. I was up the country the greater part of the time. I took a great deal of interest in the affairs of the colony from being acquainted with a great number of settlers. At that time there was a considerable scarcity of shepherds and stockmen. I consider to allow a person of small capital to become a proprietor of flocks and herds, would be beneficial to the colony if he contributed to the revenue by the payment of a licence. If squatting be allowed it will increase the export of wool, and not injure any class of settlers. It is also my impression that the natives here in the west are in a more advanced state, nearer civilisation, than I found them in New South Wales. I consider, here, if the establishment is properly managed, it is not dangerous for small squatters to go out into the bush, but if allowed to scatter, they not being able to protect their property and fatal consequences might ensue.

I do not consider a license of £20 too much.

John had given a long and detailed submission which revealed not only the extent of his travels but also the way he picked up nuggets of information like a prospector looking for his El Dorado. I have no doubt that had things turned out differently, he would have made his fortune in the great Australian outback. In many ways, he had a lot in common with Pa!

The man certainly knew how to address the Council. I suppose, what with his family background and all, he'd picked up a few tricks along the way: and being a Tipperary man, he was canny, too. Understanding that it was common knowledge that his sheep were running on land outside of Crown land, he knew damn well that Governor Hutt wouldn't tolerate that for long. So, what did Uncle John do? He got his buddies, the Drummonds, who were also running their sheep out there on Victoria Plains, to head up an 'expedition', which he then got splashed all over the local newspapers when they got back. It was a little like getting his retaliation in first!

September 18, 1842

Toodyay,

Sir, – I beg leave to acquaint you, for the information of His Excellency the Governor, that an extensive tract of grassy country, well suited for sheep-pasture, has lately been discovered by Messrs Drummond and myself about ten miles to the northward of Mr Drummond's station on the Moore River. I was unwilling to make any report until I had seen the full extent of the good land, and could with accuracy give in a description of it; but as it appears that the discovery of this country has attracted a good deal of public attention, I shall give, as well as I can recollect, a short account of it.

Having been informed by some natives that there was a large river about two days' journey to the north-west of the Moore River, we proceeded in that direction to see if such was the case. The reports proved correct and soon we come across grassy hills which stretched out before us in every direction, covered with a small herb which remains green during the summer months, and which sheep are so fond of eating.

This country appeared to be intersected by several small brooks, which were running at the time. We halted at a good spring; the natives informed us that there were several in that district. We travelled through a grassy country for about 8 or 9 miles, and then came to a sandy plain, shortly after a gum forest, and then arrived at the river, about twenty-five miles from the Moore River.

On our way home we again crossed the grassy country, which appeared to extend for fifteen miles from these large pools. I have no doubt but that there is a large extent of good land, as the country has been crossed in different directions, and found to be of the same character. No poisonous plants were seen, which adds materially to its value.

I have the honour to be, Sir,

Your obedient servant,
JOHN SCULLY,
Resident Magistrate

He'd hit the ball right back at the Governor, who now had to decide how to manage this vast new tract of land. Does he claim it as Crown land and put a price on it? Or does he charge a leasing fee for running sheep and cattle on it? And how does he police the area? John must have been smiling as he dried the ink on that letter!

TWENTY-SEVEN

*An American, an Irishman
and a Spaniard*

MED SCHOOL WAS GOING ALONG JUST FINE
and time was flying past. It seemed like only yesterday that I'd
landed in Dún Loaghaire and had unpacked my simple belongings in the upstairs room in Anglesea Road. Now here I
was in sight of becoming a doctor and getting married to the
most wonderful woman in the world. It all seemed somehow
dreamlike considering that I'd been sent over to study law
with strict instructions to head back home to help out with
the family business.

I'd changed. My understanding of the world had changed,
and my attitude towards my father had changed. The one constant in all this was dear Uncle John. These thoughts filtered
through my mind as we walked together towards All Hallows'
College on the south side of Dublin. John was very excited; he
had received word that his old friend Fra Rosendo Salvado
had arrived on a fundraising mission for his fledgling community of New Norcia, which John had helped him settle.

'I think you'll find him a fascinating fellow, Frankie. The man
knows everyone – kings, princes, popes, even the odd saint,

too! And I believe he's in regular contact with that woman from Crimea, what's her name?'

'You don't mean Florence Nightingale, do you?' I replied incredulously.

'Yes, that's the one. A nurse, I believe. Got her name in all the papers when that ghastly war was on. He's a bishop now I'm told, but he's far more interested in being abbot of his beloved Benedictines out on Victoria Plains. He should have some good stories to tell, no doubt, plus some not-so-good ones too if my friends back there are correct.'

Spring was in the air, though in Ireland that could change in a couple of hours, hence the reason for carrying brollies and heavy gabardine macs over our arms. It was a grand walk over the Liffey and on to the college. The weak sun shone on us and the fresh tinge of green haloed the hedges and the trees. Life was returning to the world.

We were greeted by Father Smythe, who was the agent for Salvado in Ireland, and shown into the parlour, where tea was arranged and a messenger sent to seek out the Spanish monk. When he arrived in the doorway I was surprised at how small he was, and slightly stout, too. Perhaps life as a missionary wasn't too unhealthy after all. He wore a full beard which had turned white long ago, and though his eyes were youthful, the creases around them belied his age.

There were hugs and laughter as the two old companions re-acquainted themselves with each other. 'And this is my nephew from America, Frankie Scully. He's almost a doctor, and he'll be a fine one, too, if I'm a good judge of character.'

Before I could say hello the good monk reached out and gripped John firmly by the arm. 'I never met a man yet who was more reliable or generous than you, John' he said.

'Your English is excellent, Your Grace', I said, leaning forward to kiss the ring on his hand.

'That's because I am English', he answered playfully. 'After all, I was made a British subject back in the forties, so that makes almost another forty years of being a loyal subject to Her Majesty, Queen Victoria.'

'It seems that I'm the only foreigner here then', I riposted.

'It won't be long before the Americans take over the world', the little Spaniard said.

Formalities over, we sat down and partook of tea and sandwiches whilst enjoying the soft heat emanating from the newly installed radiators. 'The last time I was here I nearly froze to death', he said over the edge of his teacup.

'That reminds me of the time those poor native children died in Fremantle. Do you remember that, Father?' John instantly realised that he had made an episcopal error but Salvado held up his hand to quieten his conscience.

'I never took to the role of bishop, John. You should know that. I'm much happier being a simple monk. And yes, I do remember those poor children. But if my memory serves me correctly, that happened just before I arrived. Have you told Frankie about it?'

'No', he said with a pained expression on his face. 'It's not one of those things one likes to remember too often. It was in the winter of 1843. A young Aboriginal boy had died. Not too unusual really, but this happened in the government school in Fremantle which was run by a certain Mrs Robinson. Millet was the boy's name. He was just six and had been sickly ever since he'd arrived: he'd been at the school for two years. His death was reported as being accelerated by exposure to the wet, and having an insufficiency of clothes – at least, those were the words in the official report. Mr Charles Symmonds, the Protector of Natives, interviewed the woman. According to her, there had been a storm recently and the school roof was leaking, but she thought that Millet wouldn't have been affected as he was normally put in the corner of the room. She also stated that despite him suffering chronic ill health she had had only one occasion to summon the local doctor for him! Mr Symmonds concluded that the only thing that needed to be done was to repair the leaking roof.'

The radiator knocked a couple of times in the silence that ensued.

'I remember the date because it was later that year that Bishop Brady arrived. Of course he was just plain Father Brady then. You'd remember him well, wouldn't you, Rosendo? You don't mind me calling you that within these four walls, do you?'

The nuggetty little Spaniard smiled. 'Of course not. As for Bishop Brady, how could I ever forget that man? I hear he's still alive. Do you ever hear from him, John?'

'I tried to contact him on a number of occasions, but for some reason we never actually met up. He did write me some kind words about our early times in New South Wales, but he never mentioned Perth at all.'

'Who's this Father Brady John? I remember you mentioned him once', I asked.

'We'd met briefly in Windsor when he was a curate there. Then in December '43, I got news that Father John Brady had arrived. The wool clip had just been taken down to Guildford so I headed on into the settlement to meet my old friend. He seemed mightily pleased to see a familiar face and told me all about his mission in the west. I remember that he was full of questions about the number of Catholics, the number of Aborigines, and the man seemed to be bursting with enthusiasm for the new challenge. But as we all know, sometimes enthusiasm isn't enough. The poor fellow had the zeal of a missionary but he had no idea of the opposition he was about to face from the Protestant ascendancy. In the end, I believe that it drove the poor fellow half mad.

'The paper was full of it', he went on, searching his waistcoat for his elusive pipe. 'The arrival of the first papist priest was certainly something to set the tongues wagging. But as the Good Book tells us, the man fell amongst thieves. I was well away from the settlement and only heard dribs and drabs from time to time. He was given some dubious information, the upshot of which was that he headed off to Rome to get more help, and more money of course, and that's where you come in, I think, Rosendo.'

Rosendo nodded, and began. 'He was such a simple man in many ways. Too gullible for his own good and then he couldn't bear thinking the worst of people so he took more and more of the blame upon himself. I remember visiting him one time and a small crowd had only recently left after pelting the lean-to shack that he called home with rocks. Then I came across him in the church pacing up and down, talking away to himself in a most distracted manner. When I asked him what was wrong, he just said, 'Nothing.' I think he was half mad even then.

'He left me in charge when he headed back to Rome, leaving me all alone to manage the Swan River Settlement as well as my beloved New Norcia, which was a hundred miles away. His accounts were a total mess. He was being robbed blind by his so-called advisors in whom he placed far too much trust.

Naturally I had to challenge him over it and that's when we fell out. After that, things went from bad to worse for him.'

John prodded his now glowing utensil in the Spaniard's direction. 'Do you remember when you arrived?' The two of them beamed happily at the memory.

'How could I ever forget, my friend?'

'It was you, Father Serra, the Frenchman La Fontaine, and the Irish catechist Gorman who travelled on the back of my dray up to my place at Bolgart. I remember you arriving and hoping to the good Lord that you all knew what you were taking on!'

'It took us three days in incessant heat with constant irritation from those Australian flies whilst being bumped along a terrible track. But you and your housekeeper Helen were home to greet us and I'll always be grateful for that. From there we found the site which you'd suggested and, as you'd know, it was grindingly hard work making any impression on that land. You and Helen had to rescue us on a good few occasions and if it hadn't been for your generosity and help, the mission would have failed.' The little Spaniard suddenly looked like a sad, shaggy dog and a tear appeared in the corner of his eye. 'Remember poor Gorman?'

'I never forgot him', John replied. 'In fact, I've brought along a letter I received from a colleague of La Fontaine sometime after it all happened. I thought you might be interested in reading it.' He reached into his inside jacket pocket and pulled out some flimsy sheets of paper, which he handed across to his friend. Salvado handled them as if they were a rare treasure.

'I'm not sure if I'm ready to read them, and anyhow, I've left my reading glasses up in my room. Perhaps Frankie might like to read it out aloud for me.'

'It would be an honour, Sir. Er, Father.' The two older men chuckled softly at my confusion.

From: Léandre Fontana
Perth, Swan River,
New Holland,
West Coast,

29th December 1846.

On the Saturday evening we arrived at a farm whose owner is the magistrate for this part of the colony and where it is planned to build a township upon further expansion of the colony. The territory is named Toodjay and the farm Bolgard. The owner, a former captain, is still quite young. He is a Catholic. His name is Scully. Two of his domestic servants are likewise Catholics. We were perfectly well received there. We had covered a hundred miles since Perth. We stayed on until Wednesday so as to get some rest, of which we had great need. Dom Serra and Dom Salvado celebrated Mass each day and also on the day that we resumed our journey. This latter day was Ash Wednesday. Dom Serra performed the ceremony proper to that season and set out, all with great consolation. Toodjay is the last place where Whites are to be found. From now on we would be travelling at random.

The captain had lent us his cart and his domestic servant to guide us some forty miles to a spot where the land was suitable for cultivation. We took three days to cover this distance. On the third day, at four in the afternoon, we reached the place. The land was perfectly all right but what a disappointment not to find any water! The natives had prompted us to hope for some there, but the heat of the sun had dried it all up. What could we do? We dug; we burrowed on every side, but never a drop. Ah my God, what heat! We couldn't even eat, so great was our thirst. We were without resort, especially the good young Irishman whom His Lordship had given as our companion. We didn't know which way to turn. The captain's domestic was worried about the oxen, for any return the way we had come was out of the question since the oxen were too worn out. Moreover, such return would be useless and just an added effort for them. We had not found any water for the last fifteen miles, and even there the quantity had been so small that it was scarcely sufficient for the men. We just had to resign ourselves and hope in God.

'Ah, I remember that as if it were just yesterday', Father Salvado murmured.

'Me, too', sighed John. 'Didn't you have to go back to the settlement after a month or so because you'd run out of provisions?'

'That was when I played the piano to raise some money. It went quite well if I remember correctly.'

'Quite well', expostulated John. 'If I remember accurately, the local Anglican lent you his church hall, the local Jew printed the tickets, the Sisters of Mercy provided the piano and you played for three hours non-stop after having spent five days of near starvation whilst walking back from your campsite! How much did you raise? Was it a hundred pounds?' John turned to me. 'This inconspicuous little Spaniard is a genius at music.

He wrote down the native tunes in European format. Then he taught them to play the violin as well – he even started a small orchestra of native children! And he taught them to play cricket!'

Salvado smiled, then a cloud descended on him. 'But whilst I was playing for the settlers, a tragedy was playing out in the small group I left behind.' He looked at John who understood intimately what he was talking about.

'So, what happened?' I asked naively

Father Salvado took a deep breath. 'Because I'd taken so long getting to Perth, Father Serra thought I had got lost, so he set out to find me, leaving Gorman and La Fontaine alone together.' He paused. 'It seems that as food had almost run out, La Fontaine had gone out to see if he could shoot anything and been caught out by a shower of rain, so he ran back to our temporary hut. But what does he write in his letter?'

I took up the letter again and continued reading.

> Meanwhile Mr Gorman asks me what time it is. I turn aside to answer him. 'About twelve', I say. And at that moment the gun goes off. Taken by surprise at the detonation, I cast my eyes about to see where the shot has hit. The whole blast lodges in the head of my unfortunate friend, knocking off the top of his skull and scattering the brains.
>
> Then, despite the rain, which was falling in abundance, I take the route for Bolgard, the residence of the magistrate. But scarcely have I gone fifteen yards when reflecting on how impossible it is for me to go those forty miles on my own in bush whose tracks I do not know at all, I get the idea of looking for the

shepherds who are camped three miles from our place and of placing myself in their hands. Moreover these were the magistrate's own shepherds. Thither do I run. They received me with pity and during the night they came to check on how things stood and to take care of the body, blocking the cabin door lest the wild dogs come and eat the corpse. Then, the next day, one hour after sunrise, I set out with one of them to put myself into the hands of the magistrate.

He listened to my account and to that of the man who had brought me and then pronounced that English law had no punishment for involuntary crimes. He sent off an express letter to the Colonial Secretary, along with a letter for His Lordship. For my part, I wrote to Dom Serra and I impatiently awaited his arrival, hard pressed as I was for the need for consolation and also in order to see my friend honourably buried. Dom Serra finally arrived. He received me like a criminal. My heartbreak was complete. My soul had been waiting for consolations but these were refused. I wanted to confess. It would have been a great consolation for me to go to Our Lord. The one and the other were denied me.

The college clock on the mantle shelf ticked loudly in the silence.

'The poor man', John said quietly. 'I had to take depositions from the two shepherds. According to them, when he'd gone hunting, he'd fired off just one shot and missed the game he was aiming at, which meant that there was one live shot still in the barrel. By all accounts he didn't then cock the gun to make it safe. Secondly, when he got back to the hut, Gorman had his trousers off and was repairing them. Knowing how vicious the thorns are on those scrubby bushes I can fully understand the need to repair them. The rest was as La Fontaine described. I arranged for a coffin to be sent direct to the hut so that any prowling dogs didn't attack the body, and told the shepherds to secure the cabin.'

'It was a sad and sorry affair', Salvado continued. 'So very sad. And the upshot of all that was that the mission was just down to myself and Serra, and he was sent to Rome by Brady to raise vital funds, leaving me as the last Spaniard standing.'

'As I said, Frankie, for a small man he casts a mighty shadow!'

The mood lightened after that as they talked about those early days. They'd been tough times, but it had been the same for everyone. The price of wool had fallen dramatically as had the price of the sheep themselves. The market was being flooded with cheap imports from the eastern states. Workers were leaving because of poor wages and there were increasingly fewer people to work the fields. The colony was crying out for more labour and greater access to exports. There was even talk of bringing in Chinese or Indian labour and rumours that convicts might be brought out from Britain.

Our visit to All Hallows' drew to a close. 'How long were you two guys together in Perth?' I asked.

'About six months', John said, 'but at the time it seemed like years.'

'Dear John', said Salvado, taking his friend by the arms. 'You have always remained in my prayers. Without you I would not even be here. Without you, New Norcia would never have happened.'

'And without you, Uncle John, I definitely wouldn't be here. Pa would have hounded me back to America some years back if he'd discovered how I'd been wasting my time!' The two old men smiled and then clasped each other in a hug. It was so unusual to see two grown men embracing in such a way – but it was comical, too, with the short, stout Spaniard barely coming up to the chest of his lean, old, Irish friend. But I treasured that sight.

TWENTY-EIGHT

Retribution

AS WE WALKED BACK UP GRAFTON STREET, I asked Uncle John how it had felt when he got back to Ireland. After all, it might have been tough in the colonies, but back in Ireland it was becoming diabolical. Even now, when I meet with folk in Dublin and the talk turns to the Great Hunger, you can literally feel the tension grow in the air. Jaws clench, eyes fix you with an angry stare and grown men glower into their pints as if searching for an answer to that particular horror. In just seven years, over one million people died and another million were forced to emigrate.

'I certainly knew all about it, Frankie. Mother kept me up to date with her letters and everyone in the colony was getting the same news. They were worse than desperate times. But then desperate men do desperate things.'

As if to try and change the subject, John said, 'Do you remember me telling you about the Drummond family? Well, shortly before I departed from Bolgart, John Drummond stirred things up terribly. Some thought he'd gone feral and others saw him as some sort of champion. As usual, the truth was lost somewhere in the middle of it all but it was left to me to make some sense of it all and report to the Governor.

'You might remember that John was an Inspector of police in my area and when a local Noongar speared his younger brother in retaliation for him taking his wife, Inspector John used native law to settle the issue. He tracked the Noongar down and shot him.'

'Wow', was my intelligent response. 'How come, John? I thought he was a good guy.'

'I think he probably was, but when your younger brother is killed in dubious circumstances, there's always the chance that one's objectivity might get blurred. The story I heard was that Johnston had taken an expedition to collect some plant specimens. For some reason, he'd also taken with him a local native woman, whom he was reported to be sleeping with. During the night, Kabinger, a known sheep stealer and husband of the native woman, went into their tent and speared Johnston twice in the chest, killing him. Kabinger then disappeared into the bush. When I received a report on the incident, it was my duty as magistrate to send the local policeman after the suspect to apprehend him. That policeman was John Drummond!

'John spent some weeks tracking the man down and when he caught up with him, according to the man with him, called for Kabinger to surrender. According to the report, the native then prepared to throw his spear, so John shot him dead.

'I reported all this to the Governor after I'd interviewed all the witnesses, thinking that John would get a fair hearing. What I didn't expect was that my report would be totally ignored. Someone else had whispered in the esteemed gentleman's ear that Johnston had gone to a campsite of local natives with grog in order to get the woman drunk. And according to information that only the Governor was privy to, when John had tracked the native down, he shot him in the back and killed him. The upshot was that John was suspended from duty and there was uproar amongst the settlers out at Toodyay, who supported John to a man. There was a feeling at the time that once the natives realised that the local policemen had gone then they'd be taking revenge on the white fellas right, left and centre. But that never eventuated.

'It all settled with time and John got another job up near Geraldton and I believe he's been very successful up there. As for the local natives, they continued to struggle and slowly faded as the white settlers inexorably took over their natural hunting grounds.

'Then some good news arrived in the colony and, strangely, it all happened in my neck of the woods.'

'Nothing strange about that', I interjected playfully. John glanced across at me and his face creased into a smile.

'A Mr Gregory had gone on an expedition with four horses and enough stores to last him seven weeks in the bush. He started out from Tom Yule's place and then he landed at my place. It seemed that Scully's of Bolgart was a natural wayside stop for all travellers passing through that district, so I didn't take it as anything out of the ordinary! But when the man came back, he brought news which delighted nearly all of the settlers. He'd found a seam of coal! In fact, he said that there were two seams of coal, one five feet, the next six feet thick. Apparently, they dug out about 500 weight of coal and made a fire, which, if my memory serves me correctly, the man said, "Burned perfectly, blazed brightly, and consumed entirely away to a white ash".

'It appeared that the industrial revolution which was turning the rest of the world on its head was about to hit those distant shores.'

We were getting close to Anglesea Road and John's breathing was becoming laboured with all the walking and talking. 'Why', I asked him, 'after going through all those tough times, just when things looked like taking a turn for the better, why on earth did you leave and come back to Ireland in the middle of one of the biggest natural disasters ever to plague this poor country?'

'Let's go in and have a glass of something warm and I'll tell you why then.' The dolphin on the front door shook as we closed it against a chill wind. I went into the parlour and got the small fire blazing in the grate. John appeared from the kitchen with two mugs of tea, laced no doubt with a tot of rum. 'Maria's out', he winked at me.

As we settled into our chairs I thought he was looking his age and the flesh seemed to be falling away from his face. Those blue eyes of his still seemed clear, but were red rimmed and a pale flag of tissue was sailing slowly towards his pupil. I recognised this to be a pterygium – often caused by exposure to the dry, dusty winds and the powerful sunlight found in countries like Australia.

'There was no choice, lad', he said with that honest voice of his. 'Da had had a stroke and wasn't expected to live. Ma wrote and told me and asked if I'd come home.' He paused and I thought I saw a flash of anger in his eyes.

'Would you believe that they wouldn't let me go unless I officially resigned from my position in Toodyay? They'd let others go home on compassionate leave, but for some reason … no, I know exactly for what reason they refused permission for me to leave unless I resigned from everything. That's even though I promised in writing that once I'd settled my affairs in London I would return!'

The natural silence that inhabited that cosy little parlour returned to embrace us both. 'The real reason was that I'd indicated that I was interested in the post of Colonial Secretary. Peter Broun was a sick man and George Moore had been standing in for him. And doing a good job, by the by. But when this upstart from Bogart started suggesting that he might do a better job, then suddenly official doors closed pretty rapidly. I don't blame the man. I might even have done the same thing myself. Who knows?

'So I left. I only had time to swap my farm boots for young de Courcy Lefroy's swanky silk shirt before I headed to Perth. There was a ship called the *Despatch* due to sail with produce for Ireland, so I went on board and never saw my adopted country again.

'Sam Burges looked after my affairs, which was decent of him, and leased my place to the Lefroys and others. When I'm gone it'll go to a nephew I love well.' We both sat there in the fading light watching the dancing flames lick, and then devour the black coals.

TWENTY-NINE

In good times and in bad

MARY AND I WERE TO BE MARRIED. HER grandpa had died and she'd been there to help her grandma, which was a blessing for all concerned. By now, most people in Mary's family had come to know who I was, so when I attended the funeral everyone was most welcoming. Having a Yankee 'down the country' doesn't happen too often, even in these modern times.

A couple of months after the funeral I was down visiting Mary again. We went for a walk through the laneways up near the family farm, and I asked her to marry me. I'll always remember that moment. Everything in the world seemed to come together to enhance the brilliance of the moment – the weather, the countryside, the soft breeze that played with a strand of her hair … everything. She accepted, of course, and we hugged each other as if we were trying to press our hearts into each other.

'I'll have to ask permission of your mammy', I said.

'She's up getting confession', Mary said, clasping my fingers between hers. She lifted her head and looked at me with a knowing look.

'You mean, I should ask her when her soul is pure and clean? Mary Scully, sometimes I think you have the most devious mind this side of …' She placed her finger on my lips to halt my flow. 'Yet I do believe that's one of the best ideas I've heard in a long, long time.'

I waited for Mary's mammy until she came out of the local church and walked down its well-trodden steps. She was a dear, sweet woman who'd seen enough tragedy in her own life and yet her reply was straight to the point. 'If that's what makes you and Mary happy, son, then I give you my blessing.'

I was nearing the end of my medical training and it was my intention to head back to America with Mary. I'd left Pa believing him to be a hard-hearted man. But John had taught me that there is more to a man than you can judge from the outside. I understood a little of how much he must have suffered from the loss of not one, but two loves. If I allowed myself to imagine how life would be for me without my precious Mary … just the idea of it made me slam that door in my imagination immediately. It was time to go back home and mend some of the fences that I'd kicked over all those years ago.

Having made that decision, the future became so much clearer and brighter. We both knew that our children would have more opportunity growing up in America than they would in struggling Ireland. But we also knew that it would break her mammy's heart to lose her beloved daughter. To my great surprise, brother John stepped up to the plate like the decent man he was. When we told her mammy of our intentions, he placed his arm around his mother's shoulders, saying, 'I'll always be here for you, Mammy. So will the others. Mary, you go and make a life for yourselves in America, and take our love with you.' Even I was reduced to tears by that.

But all the crying had finished by the time the wedding came. Uncle John came and stood with me, along with many dear friends from Surgeons. It was a wonderful day. We got married in Rochestown Avenue in Dún Laoghaire and had the reception at a hotel in Monkstown.

Late in the afternoon, John and I were on the terrace of the hotel.

'Find anything interesting in those old cuttings?' he asked.

'As Mary's mammy would say, there's eating and drinking in them!'

He smiled. 'It certainly had its ups and downs. But that was in the past. You and Mary are the future. You're a married man now, Frankie, and you'd best get back to your new bride.'

'Of course, John', I replied. I was feeling sad at the thought of leaving him because I'd come to love and admire the man. In a weak attempt at humour I said, 'And don't forget to dance with that bridesmaid, I think she has her eye on you!' I pointed to one of Mary's cousins.

'If this were York forty years ago, you'd have to strap me to a bullock cart to stop me. Go on, lad. Get back to your bride.' I patted him on the shoulder and went in search of the new Mrs Scully.

Mary and I sailed the following week. I never saw Uncle John again. He died a few months later, and as promised, he left his property in Australia to his loved and loving nephew.

APPENDIX :

The loss of John Scully's inheritance

JOHN SCULLY RETURNED TO IRELAND IN January 1847. His father had died and left him a significant inheritance in the Tipperary Bank, but that was soon to change.

John Sadlier (1813-1856) – A Very Sad Liar
Turtle Bunbury - Hero's & Villains

WWW.TURTLEBUNBURY.COM/HISTORY/HISTORY_
HEROES/HIST_HERO_SADLIER.HTML

John Sadlier is arguably the best known of the Irish fraudsters who came to prominence in the Victorian Age. Banking was in his blood. His mother's father James Scully established a bank in Tipperary town in 1803. Raised a Catholic and educated at Clongowes, John Sadlier's professional career began when he succeeded his uncle to a prosperous solicitor's practice in Dublin.

In 1838, he founded the Tipperary Joint Stock Bank with his uncle James Scully as chairman. They focused on small farmers, tradesmen and clerks, offering above average interest rates. The bank prospered and by 1845 there were nine branches in operation, extending north from Tipperary into Thomastown (Co Kilkenny), Athy and Carlow.

When James Scully died in 1847, John invited his elder brother James Sadlier to become Managing Director. John was elected Liberal MP for Carlow that same year, with Captain William McClintock Bunbury representing the Conservatives. Sadlier took to politics in a seemingly calm, wise and practical manner. But behind those calculating eyes was a cold and rascally soul.

In 1848, Sadlier was appointed chairman of the London and County Joint Stock Banking Company, a post he retained until his death. Now a resident of London, he was perfectly poised to expand his networking into Europe. He began financing railway developments in Sweden, France and Italy. In 1851, he founded his own Dublin newspaper, *The Weekly Telegraph*. He purchased vast swathes of land, valued at over £250,000,000, and including the beleaguered Earl of Glengall's estate at Cahir. But for all that he lived a rather frugal life. His only flamboyance was a stable in Watford from where he hunted with the Gunnersbury hounds.

Sadlier's financial success made him a household name in the 1850s and much talk was made over his reputed wealth. He seemed to have the Midas touch; every venture he turned to came up trumps.

The shareholders were delighted. They were being paid a dividend of 6 percent, a point or two more than their competitors.

In 1851, the Liberal Government attempted to restructure the Catholic Church in England, a move which would inevitably undermine the Vatican's influence. Sadlier, an ardent Catholic, led the opposition to the legislation; his supporters became known as the Pope's Brass Band. That same year, Sadlier helped establish the Catholic Defence Association. When the Liberals returned to power in late 1852, the 'brilliant' Sadlier accepted a post as a Junior Lord of the Treasury.

However, unbeknownst to everyone, the Sadliers were on very thin ice. The impression that they were flourishing was a grand illusion. The payment of high dividends was justified by fraudulent book-keeping which, for instance, falsely claimed the bank had reserves of £17,000.

The darkness began to fall in 1853 when Sadlier was forced to resign his seat, following an investigation into his 1852 election campaign. Pressure had seemingly been brought to bear by the Joint Stock Bank in Carlow upon 208 voters in the constituency. The word was out that Sadlier's wizardry was not as magical as it might seem.

As Sadlier's fortunes began to sink, he resorted to increasingly wild speculations and illicit tactics. He began to borrow heavily from his own bank. He began courting Catholic heiresses and proposing marriage to them. The bachelor began to forge shares in the Royal Swedish Railway Company, of which he was chairman.

On 13 February 1856, the London agents of the Tipperary Bank refused to cash drafts sent to them by Sadlier. The following weekend, the depressed and bloated banker wrote a letter of grief and remonstrance to a cousin, confessing to the 'numberless crimes of a diabolical character' which had caused 'ruin and misery and disgrace to thousands – nay, tens of thousands'. His body was found on Hampstead Heath on the Sunday morning, alongside a silver cream jug and a vial of poisonous prussic acid.

It transpired that his personal overdraft had climbed to £250,000. His collapsed banking empire also owed the Bank of Ireland £122,000. His depositors, the farmers and labourers, lost £70,000. Considering that the amount of deposits in all the Joint Stock Banks in Ireland was only £12,000,000 at that time, a loss of £400,000 in four counties was a very heavy calamity. He had also defrauded the Royal Swedish Railway Company of £300,000.

Ireland was stunned. The press called him the 'Prince of Swindlers', a miser 'wrinkled with multifarious intrigue, cold, callous and cunning'. Charles Dickens may have had a greater role in immortalising him in Little Dorrit, published in 1857, in which the character Mr Merdle was based on Sadlier.

Sadlier's brother James did not live happily ever after. He was expelled from the House of Commons and fled to Zurich where he was murdered while walking one day in 1811.

After the failure of the bank and the loss of his inheritance, John found himself in difficult circumstances. Luckily, his youngest brother Francis, who was an MP in London, had some influence with the authorities in Dublin. He secured a position for his elder brother as Resident Magistrate in Oughterard, County Galway, where John lived until the early 1880s.

John Scully married Maria MacDermott on 15 September 1851. They had no children. He died on 26 June 1890 in Anglesea Road, County Dublin.

ABOUT THE AUTHOR

"I spent all my life learning the rules. Now that I know which ones are irrelevant, life is simpler!"

AFTER MORE THAN thirty years as a busy family practice physician in Perth, Duncan Jefferson retired from his practice and started traveling. He still practices medicine part time, as a relief doctor traveling to the most remote corners of Australia, and in between assignments he and his wife travel the world.

Duncan has walked the famous Camino de Santiago, and now volunteers his time as the chairman of The Pilgrim

Trail Foundation, which is organizing a similar, contemplative-style walk in Australia called the Camino Salvado.

VISIT HIM ONLINE AT

WWW.DUNCANJEFFERSON.COM